MRS. POLLIFAX, INNOCENT TOURIST

MRS. POLLIFAX,
INNOCENT
TOURIST

DOROTHY GILMAN

DOUBLEDAY DIRECT LARGE PRINT EDITION
FAWCETT COLUMBINE • NEW YORK

A Fawcett Columbine Book
Published by Ballantine Books

Copyright © 1997 by Dorothy Gilman Butters

All rights reserved under International and Pan-American Copyright Conventions. Published in the United States by Ballantine Books, a division of Random House, Inc., New York, and simultaneously in Canada by Random House of Canada Limited, Toronto.

ISBN 1-56865-321-2

Printed in the United States of America

**This Large Print Book carries the
Seal of Approval of N.A.V.H.**

1

Carstairs was seated at his desk at headquarters, yawning over an intelligence report laden with statistics, when Bishop opened the door and announced that John Sebastian Farrell was asking to see him.

Startled, Carstairs said, "*Our* Farrell?"

"Ours *once,* yes."

"Good heavens! Perhaps we can persuade him to—send him in, Bishop."

"No, you can't persuade me to sign up again," said Farrell, over Bishop's shoulder, and he walked boldly in, as insouciant as ever. "I've come for information, as well as to rob you of one of your more valuable commodities, so to speak."

"You terrify me," Carstairs told him with a smile. "Damn good to see you again,

Farrell. I'd like to think your art gallery in Mexico City has begun to bore you—I have my fantasies—but pull up a chair and I'll ask Bishop to bring some coffee."

"I've already asked for coffee," Farrell told him, seating himself in the chair next to his desk. "Cheeky of me, of course—and I should have telephoned first, but after flying up from Mexico City yesterday to New York, and this morning from New York to—" He stopped as Bishop brought in two coffees and placed them on Carstairs's desk. "Thanks, Bishop."

"Go on," said Carstairs.

Farrell smiled pleasantly. "I'm here to ask if you've heard of a man named Antun Mahmoud. Publishes some sort of newspaper—in Arabic—in Manhattan."

Carstairs gave him a long look and said curtly, "Yes, but I'm surprised that *you've* heard of him."

"Is he reliable? Can he be trusted?"

Carstairs's eyes narrowed. "I'd like to know first just how you've heard of him."

"That sub rosa, hmmm?" murmured Farrell, looking pleased. "It explains what struck me as a bad case of paranoia."

Carstairs said sharply, "You've met the man?"

"Yes, last night in Manhattan. As soon as the plane landed, I called the number he'd given me."

"If you could enlighten me as to what this is all about . . ." began Carstairs.

Farrell said simply, "It concerns Dib Assen."

"Dib Assen," repeated Carstairs, startled. "You were friends, I know. I read of his death, was it a month ago? 'DISSIDENT IRAQI AUTHOR DIES IN PRISON.' "

Farrell nodded. "I'd known him for years, ever since he came here to lecture at Columbia on Islamic culture, art, and literature. We kept in touch, and God knows I tried to persuade him to move to America before it was too late, but he only laughed at the idea. However, I did extract one promise from him, namely to let me know if I could be of help in any way and at any time."

Carstairs's brows lifted. "And?"

Farrell said quietly, "There is a manuscript—safely hidden away before he was arrested. One of his friends in Iraq pledged to him that the manuscript would be smuggled out of the country to me, and only to me personally, should he die. To be delivered to his publishers."

"I see," murmured Carstairs.

"The friend's name is Ibrahim—no last name—and I was contacted by these people in Manhattan—this Antun Mahmoud—to say that Ibrahim hopes, *In-sha'Allah,* to meet me in Amman, Jordan, between the tenth of October and the thirteenth. And this is the seventh."

Carstairs whistled faintly. "Doesn't give you much time."

"No," agreed Farrell, "but you can imagine his difficulties in getting out of Iraq. Presumably it means he's made it."

"Presumably, yes," said Carstairs. "And you want to know if these New York people can be trusted."

"Definitely. If you could know what I had to go through, being interrogated by this Antun Mahmoud, not to mention where he took me! The most godawful place in the most godawful neighborhood. I also gave him rather a lot of money to arrange things."

Carstairs smiled. "He can be trusted, yes. . . . I won't tell you the position he held in Iraq before he fled the country, but he's important enough to still be a threat to them. In fact, since he came to the United States, we know of two assassination attempts on his life. . . . Saddam is not forgiving! The newspaper that Antun Mahmoud and his group publish is a monthly newsletter for fellow exiles. We believe their closest connection is with the Arab Organization for Human Rights. I must admit that we envy their news-gathering sources." He shrugged. "Once in a while they feed us information, but they'll have nothing to do with us in general, and we respect their resolve."

"Well, that's a relief," said Farrell. "But I have to add my second reason for being here. I insisted to them that I have 'cover.' They don't much like that, but something about this feels as shaky as—well, Jell-O. Especially when, at the last minute, it was pointed out to me that I'd have to keep returning for three or four mornings to the same meeting place."

"What meeting place?"

"They will give me that information to-morrow night, but I mean: if Ibrahim's late, a solitary American tourist hanging around some obscure corner of Amman? Damned conspicuous!" Watching Carstairs, he said firmly, "I insisted on a companion. An Innocent Tourist, eminently respectable, a woman, for instance, who wears outrageous hats and knows karate."

Carstairs grinned. "I see. Mrs. Pollifax, of course."

"Yes, do you mind? I mean, old chap, she does work for you, technically. I'd like to borrow her. *If,* of course, she can leave with me tomorrow night for Jordan, following that final briefing by Antun."

"Jordan," mused Carstairs. "This Ibrahim has a terrible desert and dangerous borders to cross. Did whatever message reached Antun say that the man *hoped* to reach Amman by the tenth, or that he was already there?"

Farrell sighed. "I believe the word was 'expected'. I might also add that Antun Mahmoud's not at all happy about the Duchess—Mrs. Pollifax, that is—going with me; he insists on meeting her, too, before plane-time, which is nine P.M. tomorrow."

"She can't be seen entering their

place," Carstairs pointed out sharply. "Even I don't know where they are just now."

Farrell nodded. "I'll think of a disguise of some sort. And thanks."

Carstairs flicked a switch on his intercom. "Bishop—"

"Yes, sir?"

"Get Mrs. Pollifax on the phone, Farrell hopes to borrow her if she's available."

Bishop's voice was cheerful. "She ought to be available, sir, I spoke with her only a few days ago. You recall young Kadi Hopkirk?"

"Indeed yes."

"Cyrus is introducing her to bird-watching; I believe they're still at the Cape. Cape Cod."

"Mrs. Pollifax too?"

"She said she doesn't enjoy crouching in marshes for hours, not after her experience in Albania."

Farrell chuckled. "Lake Scutari! I was with her, you know. We spent an entire night floating around that damn lake, clinging to a log."

Over the intercom Bishop laughed. "And she still smelled of goat in spite of it.

Come to my office and we'll see if she's at home."

As Farrell rose from his chair, Carstairs said curtly, "Just a minute."

Farrell waited, brows lifted questioningly.

"I think we'd like to see that novel by Dib Assen if you get hold of it."

Farrell smiled. "I thought history was your passion. I didn't know you read novels."

Carstairs hesitated. "There's one thing I guess you'd better know before you go charging off on this quixotic mission of yours. A word of warning, so to speak."

"Yes?"

"Until a few years ago Dib Assen not only wrote his novels, he did some work for us."

Farrell's jaw dropped. "I don't believe it."

"Try. I'm certain your friend Antun Mahmoud doesn't know, but it may—just *may*—have been learned in Baghdad. It could possibly be why he was imprisoned this time—he's been arrested before—but this time *not* released. They had time to make him talk, didn't they?"

Farrell winced. "And you're trying to say . . ."

Carstairs nodded. "I'm trying to say that his novel may not be entirely a novel. If so—and there are many ifs here, Farrell—there could be others interested in it if Assen was forced to talk before he died, or if somehow it became known that a man is smuggling some of his papers out of Iraq. Still want to hazard your mission?"

Farrell said flatly, "I owe Dib Assen, I've told you that, but whether I should take the Duchess—"

Carstairs said dryly, "You'll need her more than ever, I'd say. Who on earth would suspect *her*? She can also keep an eye on you. . . . Now go and see if Bishop's reached her on the phone—and good luck to you."

W hen the phone rang Mrs. Pollifax was seated at her desk writing a letter, a lost art form that she still cherished and which was certainly practical in this case, when the letter was addressed to an old friend in Europe named Robin Burke-Jones and she had so much to say. The mail that she received from exotic out-of-the-way places of the earth mystified the postman, and it would have shocked him to learn that when she'd first met Robin he was a jewel thief, and that his talents were now devoted to Interpol. Mrs. Pollifax, with her prize-winning geraniums, her lectures at the Garden Club, her marriage to Cyrus— a retired judge—was the last person to be suspected of consorting with thieves, spies, and murderers.

Which, of course, was why she had proven of considerable value to Carstairs of the CIA.

She was just addressing the envelope when the phone rang, and picking up the receiver, she was astonished to hear Farrell's voice. "Duchess," he said, "I need you. I'm calling from Carstairs's office, and he says I can borrow you if you're free to fly to Jordan tomorrow night."

"T-tomorrow night?" she stammered. "Jordan? The Jordan that's in the Middle East?"

"I know it's sudden," he said, "but if you're free to go with me tomorrow, I can be with you this afternoon and explain why—if you'll just say you're free for about five or six days."

She said doubtfully, "I'm free, yes, but what—"

"Good. Brew some coffee for me, I'm flying back to New York where I'll rent a car and arrive about two o'clock."

He hung up, leaving her dazed, curious, interested, and then oddly excited. Jordan . . . the Middle East? What did she know about the country except that it was surrounded by Israel, Syria, Iraq, and Saudi Arabia, where all sorts of dramatic events appeared to happen? A lunch, however, remained a necessity, and leaving her envelope unstamped she proceeded to postpone looking at maps and made sandwiches.

She had accomplished a great deal when Farrell drove up to the house and climbed out of a shiny red car. *Still the same ex-CIA adventurer,* she thought, regarding him with affection as he bounded up the steps toward her: a little too handsome for his own good, his tanned face a shade more hardened since that first meeting some years ago, when—on her first assignment from Carstairs and fresh from her Garden Club—she had been appalled to find herself tied back to back with such a man in a dim shack in Mexico.

"Come in and talk," she told him, giving him a hug. "Although why you need me—"

"As cover," he told her, with the flash of a smile. "You're not insulted that it's nothing more dangerous? My intuition tells me it's a damn good idea, but I don't know why."

"Then you're turning into a Carstairs, it must be contagious," she said. "*He* seems to operate most of the time on intuition. But why the Middle East? And if you're still not with the CIA—"

"No, but I needed some information from Carstairs, and I still feel obligated to clear it with him when I want to borrow you. He sends greetings."

"But your art gallery in Mexico City?"

He made a face. "Since the peso plummeted I've placed it on hold. And my going to Jordan has nothing to do with the CIA, it's a debt of honor to an old, very good friend."

"Tell me," she said, bringing him coffee and a tuna fish sandwich.

He was silent a moment, and then, "Okay, it's like this, Duchess. I have a friend—*had* a friend," he amended. "He came to the United States some years ago to lecture on the Middle East at Columbia. He was a scholar, gifted and intelligent, and an Iraqi. In those days Saddam Hussein had only begun rearranging the country and seemed of little importance. My friend lectured on Islam and the Arab world, its literature, drama, culture, art, and its escape from the Colonial powers."

"And you met him in New York."

Farrell nodded. "We became friends, good friends. I'd done some intelligence work in the Middle East, I was quite frank about that. He returned to Iraq to continue writing the books he wanted to write." He hesitated, and then, "Only two of his books have been published in this country. Angry ones. Have you heard of the author Dib Assen?"

Mrs. Pollifax frowned. "Dib Assen . . . I don't think—" She gave a start. "No, wait, I did read a book, *Plague of Demons,* a devastating satire on life under a nameless dictator, and it was written by an

Iraqi. Quite unforgettable. Could that have been Dib Assen?"

Farrell nodded. "That was Dib Assen, yes. His second novel published in English was titled *Instruments of Torture,* supposedly about a love affair but actually a dangerous piece of political work."

"Go on . . ."

"We corresponded. I'd written him of my worries for him after he was first arrested and released. He said he wrote what he must, and he continued, much of his later work being circulated underground in manuscript form. By then I had promised—pledged to him—that if ever he needed help, he could depend on me."

Mrs. Pollifax nodded. "And now he needs help."

"No, unfortunately, because he's dead," Farrell told her bluntly. "The London papers carried the most extensive obituary; his death was reported as a heart attack, and they uncovered the fact that he died in their vilest prison, the Ba'thi Iraq. Do you believe he died of a heart attack?"

"No, poor soul," she said. "Not if he

continued writing books like *Plague of De-mons.*"

"He never stopped," said Farrell, "and now there is one last manuscript, appar-ently hidden away just before his arrest. A friend of his in Baghdad was given my name long ago, and he promised to de-liver the manuscript to me, trusting no one else. This courageous friend of his is named Ibrahim. No last name. And for me this is a responsibility, Duchess, a grave and important one. A debt of honor. I can't fail him."

"But—how on earth were you con-tacted?" she asked. "How did you hear of and from this Ibrahim?"

Farrell grinned. "You'll have to meet the people arranging this trip and pass their inspection, Duchess. There are Iraqi exiles in Manhattan who somehow, through mysterious channels, pick up bits and pieces of news and publish a newsletter, and it was through them that I heard of this Ibrahim. They don't relish at all my in-sistence that you accompany me. The plane leaves tomorrow at nine P.M., and we have an appointment to meet them earlier. To collect tickets, added information, and for them to check you out, so to speak.''

''Of course I'll go,'' murmured Mrs. Pollifax. ''I'm not sure how to reach Cyrus by phone; I'll have to leave a message at his motel. Six days, you think? What will I need to bring?''

''Only yourself, looking as innocent and touristy as possible. And your passport—if you'll give it to me now, I'll stop at the Jordanian Consulate in New York and have it visa-stamped; you'll need that for entry.''

Recovering her passport from a desk drawer she handed it to him, and he opened it and grinned. ''Emily Reed-Pollifax . . . We still assume some responsibility for this marriage, you know. After all, if we'd not sent you off to Zambia—just think!—you might never have met your dashing Cyrus Reed.''

''That,'' said Mrs. Pollifax with a twinkle, ''is why I still send you a fruitcake every Christmas.''

Farrell laughed. Tucking away her passport he hesitated and then added apologetically, ''There's one other matter. . . . It's unfortunate, but where I'm taking you tomorrow evening for inspection you'll need to go in a suitable disguise."

"Disguise!" she exclaimed. "Are you serious? In New York City? Good heavens, why?"

"To protect *them,* not us, Duchess," he said. "There are political assassinations even in New York: someone pushed in front of a subway train, hit by a car, or shot in an alley with all ID removed. They're frequently watched."

She said in horror, "By the CIA?"

He shook his head.

"The FBI?"

He said gently, "No, Duchess, by *them.*"

She wanted to say, *But this is America, Farrell,* but caught herself in time, realizing that America was no longer immune to terrorism and bombs.

With a glance at his wrist watch Farrell put down his cup of coffee and rose. "I'll meet you tomorrow at Grand Central station," he said quietly. "By the information booth at four-thirty P.M. The plane leaves at nine." Leaning over he kissed her cheek. "Thanks, Duchess, and remember me to Cyrus."

Before she could ask any more questions, he had picked up his briefcase and was at the door. "Remember, four-thirty P.M. tomorrow," he said. The door opened and closed behind him, and he was gone, leaving her to meditate upon a world gone mad and a mysterious Iraqi exile whom she was to meet tomorrow.

But this was today. She must at once devise a message for Cyrus that wouldn't worry him, and dare she mention Jordan, when he had always longed to see its ancient city of Petra? She must pack clothes and call Mr. Lupacik about looking after the house while it was empty. . . . She sighed, and then realized that at last she could wear—and at this thought she brightened—her daring new hat with its garden of pink and yellow roses.

2

The sign over the shop read WILKINS REFINING COMPANY, INC., a shabby sign on a shabby Manhattan street. On the window below, a second sign in gilt letters promised HIGHEST PRICES PAID FOR GOLD AND SILVER.

The bag lady, pushing a wire grocery cart full of plastic bags and empty cola cans, glanced up at the sign and hesitated; the man following her at a distance quickened his step, reached her side, opened the door to the refining shop, and held it wide. The man, the cart, and the woman disappeared, swallowed up by the dark interior; the door closed behind them, leaving the street empty.

Once inside the dark shop Mrs. Pollifax relaxed her grip on the cart and said crossly, "I can't help but worry about lice, Farrell. This is the most embarrassing disguise I've ever worn, I feel I should apologize to every genuine bag lady in the city."

"You've been getting spoiled, Duchess," he told her. "You came out of Albania crawling with lice, didn't you? Relax."

"Yes, but where *are* these mysterious people? There's nobody here, Farrell."

"Probably making sure we weren't followed or seen entering."

This was certainly a very educational evening, reflected Mrs. Pollifax, remembering the cheap rent-by-the-hour hotel to which Farrell had taken her, where he had amassed a collection of old clothes: a ragged trench coat, sneakers, and two worn sweaters to wear over her traveling clothes, their suitcases buried under the plastic bags and cola tins in the cart. The room had smelled of antiseptic and cheap perfume, and a flashing neon light outside the window had bathed the walls in red. It had amused her to speculate on just what Cyrus might have said if he'd seen his wife as a bag lady navigating a grocery cart down mean streets.

The silence was broken by the sound of heavy footsteps on the floor above, followed by a door closing and the opening of a door at the end of the hall beyond the shop's counter. The man silhouetted against the light behind him said, "Come in. . . . Quickly, please."

Mrs. Pollifax pushed her grocery cart with alacrity, Farrell leading the way. They entered a windowless room garishly lit by fluorescent tubes on the ceiling and empty of furniture except for a desk, four chairs, and a copying machine. The two men seated at the desk wore black business suits, white shirts, and ties, and neither looked particularly foreign. Both had black mustaches that were possibly the most luxurious she had ever seen, and both had tan complexions, but there were distinct differences. Mrs. Pollifax knew immediately, for instance, that the older man was Antun Mahmoud even before Farrell introduced him. From his bearing and the shrewdness of his glance he could have been a general—as perhaps he had once been, she reflected; she judged him to be efficient, intelligent, impatient, and wary.

His companion was an imitation of him but younger, softer.

Both looked at her appraisingly.

"Sit," said Antun sternly.

Mrs. Pollifax abandoned her cart and sat. Antun's companion, however, gave her a shy smile.

Antun peered at her, frowning. "Mr. Farrell gives you a high recommendation. You work for the CIA?"

"Occasionally they've found me useful," she said.

"Yes, but you simply don't look—"

Farrell interrupted to say curtly, "She's experienced, trust me. Duchess, peel away those layers down to your Macy's suit and rescue that incredible-looking hat from its plastic bag."

Mrs. Pollifax sighed and walked to the grocery cart, where she removed the ragged raincoat and the two threadbare sweaters to display a trim navy blue suit. Digging into the grocery cart she extracted one plastic bag, opened it, and removed from it the garden of yellow and pink roses laced to a wide brim of straw. When it was placed on her head she at once became what Carstairs of the CIA called with amusement his Very Innocent Tourist, and if the hat appeared to astonish the two men, it also appeared to explain her presence and to satisfy them.

"Ah yes, very good," said Antun, nodding. "I understand. You have passports and visas?"

"All set," Farrell told him, "except for where we meet this Ibrahim. You said mornings?"

Antun nodded. "He will look for you at Karak castle, about eighty miles south of Amman, very old, near the town of Karak. You will need a guide since you don't speak Arabic."

"A guide? Will he be—er—one of you?" asked Mrs. Pollifax.

She had offended him. He said mockingly, " 'One of us?' No. Like any tourist we consulted a Manhattan travel agency. If you don't like this one—he will meet you at the airport—there is a list of four others. Hassan, give her the list."

"Thank you," Mrs. Pollifax said meekly, and pocketed the list. "And do I leave here dressed as I came, in the old raincoat?"

He said impatiently, "No, no, someone

else will leave by the front door in those clothes, wheeling the cart and accompanied by a man. The two of you leave from the rear; there is a van waiting in the garage behind us." To Farrell he said, "This guide—his name is Youseff Jidoor—will meet you at Queen Alida Airport, holding up a sign saying Jidoor Tours."

"Shoes," said Farrell, pointing. "Duchess, you're still in sneakers. It grows late, the plane—?"

Antun nodded. "Fayad drives. You will be on time. If you are followed, Fayad is an expert at losing anyone interested."

Curious, Mrs. Pollifax said, "Are you really watched?"

Antun looked amused. "Sometimes—in the dark—one can see a cigarette carelessly lit in the supposedly empty room across the street." He reached into the drawer of the desk and drew out two envelopes. "Here are your plane tickets," he said, handing one to Farrell. "I am sorry the seats are not together, but since your insistence on this woman going with you came too late for us, such an arrangement was impossible." He gave Mrs. Pollifax the second envelope, adding, "And so, as we say, *Allah yesellimak.*"

"What does that mean?" asked Mrs. Pollifax.

"God preserve you."

"God preserve you, too," she said politely.

The van had darkened windows, and the driver, Fayad, said only, "No worry!" The garage doors swung open and they shot out into the dark street like a stone released from a slingshot.

Only now did Mrs. Pollifax think to ask, "How long is the flight ahead of us to Amman, Jordan?"

Farrell sighed. "I hoped you'd never ask," he said. "We fly all night to Amsterdam, land there in the morning for refueling and passengers, and arrive in Amman sometime after lunch. Fourteen hours, roughly."

"Fourteen hours," she repeated in shock. "Oh dear, I *never* sleep on planes, you know, which means I'll be jet-lagged out of my head, Farrell. I nap, but briefly, and that's not *real* sleep."

"No," he admitted, "but on the other hand, I'll feel free to come and talk to you—tell a few jokes—during the small hours of the night."

"But I do wish we had seats together," she said wistfully. "I'll probably be seated next to a crying child or someone who will fall asleep on my shoulder, which is always so difficult."

Actually, once boarded, Mrs. Pollifax found herself in a seat in the rear and on the aisle, next to a rather plump, well-dressed man with a *Wall Street Journal* on his lap. He did not look at all the sort who would fall asleep on her shoulder; he rose at once to help her stow her carry-on bag under the seat and said admiringly, "Please—I congratulate you on your hat, it is very beautiful, like a garden."

"Thank you," she said, removing it and tucking it on top of her carry-on bag.

"Are you traveling to the Middle East?" he inquired cordially.

"Yes, to Jordan."

Beaming, he said, "Ah—*my* country. You will visit Jerash? Petra? Wadi Rum? The Dead Sea?"

Since she had not had time to do any

research about Jordan, she sidestepped this query. "You're Jordanian, then?"

Their departure was being announced, and he fastened his seat belt. His face was round and affable, if slightly jowly. A receding hairline was compensated by a sleek black mustache. Fiftyish, she decided, and quite Savile Row in his dark suit, white tie, and white shirt.

"Ah yes, but I get off in Amsterdam in the morning," he explained. "My business is there, the making of facsimilies of Jordanian antiquities for the tourists in Jordan to carry home with them."

"You mean copies?" she suggested.

He gave her a pitying glance. "On the contrary, they are works of art and sell *very* well. Jordan is being discovered—you see how crowded the plane is?"

It was indeed crowded, every seat taken, with Farrell up front, near the movie screen, while she and this gentleman occupied seats in the very last row. Many of the passengers looked Middle Eastern, with the exception of one rather large tourist group making a great deal of noise.

"We are airborne!" announced her companion triumphantly, and with a bow of his head, he introduced himself. "I am Mr. Nayef. And you?"

"Mrs. Pollifax."

"So strange a name! Pollifax?" When she nodded, he added, "Perhaps you are part of that tour group?" He waved a hand toward the noisy Americans still calling back and forth to one another. "No? How brave you American women are—and so free! You have friends, then, in Amman?"

"No," said Mrs. Pollifax, wishing he would attend to his *Wall Street Journal* so that she could, in turn, bring out the travel guide that Farrell had loaned her.

"But allow me to advise you, then," he said firmly. "You must above all see Petra, our famous rose red city, carved out of rock so long ago." Reaching under the seat for his attaché case, he said, "I show you what I make in my factory studio in Amsterdam. Not the *El Khazna*—the great treasury building—but this also is at Petra, a rendering of the Urn Tomb."

What he handed her struck Mrs. Pollifax at first glance as a rather cheap and amateur-looking rectangle of thick plywood, to which a label had been affixed to inform in

both English and Arabic, "Urn Tomb. Petra. Nabataean. Executed by Hassur Aid."

"Turn it over," he told her reproachfully.

"Sorry," she said, and was more pleasantly surprised by the other side. Mounted
on the wooden plaque was a miniature
landscape carved in three dimensions in
polished white stone or plaster and ce-
mented to the plywood. It portrayed a
mountain of rock, each of its seams
clearly defined by the artist's knife; in the
center of the rock face was an entrance
into the mountain, guarded by two columns that rose above a colonnade with a
line of arched openings.

"Polished white limestone—and by
hand," emphasized Mr. Nayef, and leaning closer he confided, "If you would like
to buy? In Jordan this would sell for sixty
dinar, nearly one hundred U.S. dollar. I let
you have it for half."

"Quite a salesman," she told him with a
smile. "Thank you, but my carry-on bag is
full enough. I'll certainly look forward
to seeing Petra—and the Urn Tomb,
though."

"You will enjoy Amman, too," he said,

putting away the plaque. "It is built on seven hills, you know? Like Rome?"

He did not wait for a response. A very small country, Jordan, he continued, mostly desert. There were still too many refugee camps, the Bedouin were very loyal to the king, who had survived many years despite too many wars, but the schools were free and the Jordan Valley green and fertile. . . .

By the time the dinner cart made its way up the aisle Mrs. Pollifax dared to hope that he might stop talking, but he droned on as they sat side by side eating dinner: about the influx of Palestinians, some very rich, some trapped in refugee camps. Playfully he suggested that she learn to pronounce *As salam alaikum,* which meant "May peace be with you," and in turn she must respond *Alaikum as salam,* and once she had mastered this he said, beaming, "*Taib! Taib!* which means 'good.' "

At this point Mrs. Pollifax firmly ended the conversation.

"I am going to brush my teeth," she announced, and delving into her carry-on bag, she extracted toothbrush, toothpaste, washcloth, and cold cream, and left him.

When she returned Mr. Nayef was wearing earphones and was intently absorbed in the film being shown on the screen; after only the briefest of smiles he returned to the movie. Mrs. Pollifax closed her eyes and pretended to sleep, thus missing the film, but determined to prevent any further lectures once it ended.

Presently, Mr. Nayef slept, and Mrs. Pollifax alternately napped and read a magazine and soon discovered that she had been wrong about Mr. Nayef: as his head sank lower and lower, she found him asleep against her shoulder. Farrell, making his rounds during the night, grinned and said, "Men do like your shoulder!" and later brought her a fresh magazine to read. The sky began to brighten, breakfast was served, and they landed in Amsterdam; at which point Mr. Nayef stirred and began to gather up his coat and his attaché case. "Amsterdam at last!" he exclaimed, and to Mrs. Pollifax, "It has been such a pleasure talking with you."

Talking at *me,* she thought bitterly.

"And to you I now say *As salam alaikum,* and you will please say—?"

She sighed. *"Alaikum as salam."*

"Taib! Taib!" he said. "I bid you farewell."

And with that he departed, and with his departure Mrs. Pollifax assumed—quite erroneously—that she had seen the last of the tiresome Mr. Nayef.

3

It was nearly half-past four in the afternoon when they emerged from a seemingly endless line at customs. Baggage in hand they made their exodus past swarms of people waiting behind ropes, peering anxiously at each passenger, occasionally shouting and waving as friend or family emerged.

It was with some relief that Mrs. Pollifax spotted a sign, JIDOOR TOURS, held high above the crowd; she pointed and waved, Farrell waved, and from under the sign appeared a young man. An attractive young man: a well-shaped face with twin slashes of thick brows over gray eyes so light they looked almost silver in his dark face. There was also what appeared to be the ubiquitous Middle Eastern black mustache over a generous mouth. He wore a dark blue zip-up jacket over a white shirt and black slacks. Seeing Mrs. Pollifax and Farrell, he smiled and pointed, and they met at the end of the ropes that contained the crowds.

Apparently their names had not been given to him for he said, "Welcome to Amman. My name is Youseff Jidoor, but please call me Joseph—and your names?"

His excellent English was a pleasing surprise. Farrell shook his hand, saying, "This is Mrs. Pollifax, otherwise referred to as the Duchess, and I'm Farrell."

"A pleasure, a pleasure," he told them with a flash of white teeth against his tan skin. "My car is outside, shall we go now? This is your luggage?" He picked up their two suitcases and led them out into the street. "I have reserved two rooms for you at the Continental, is that okay?"

Farrell and Mrs. Pollifax exchanged glances. "It sounds a bit posh," she told him. "We go dutch on this, I insist, Farrell. Remember the plunge of the peso!"

He laughed. "Thank you but no, Duchess. My own paintings are selling very well in Arizona and Texas galleries, and I still restore old paintings. My bank account is quite solid these days, but nice of you to offer." To Joseph he said, "Have they mentioned to you that I'm here to meet a man who may be delayed?"

Joseph looked at him wonderingly. "No, Mr. Farrell."

"We may have to spend a few mornings at Karak castle, wherever that is, since the day to meet was not specific."

"How interesting." Joseph nodded. "I will see to it that we take a lunch each day for what you call a picnic." He led them to a yellow taxi. "This is my car."

"A taxi!" exclaimed Mrs. Pollifax.

Joseph said very seriously, "I am just out of university, and when there are no tourists to guide I am a taxi driver. But," he hastened to assure them, "I am a very *good* guide, I took history in university, as well as literature, and have been a guide for one year now. Once at the hotel we can speak of plans for tomorrow?"

"Perfect," said Mrs. Pollifax, climbing into the car.

The sun was not shining, which surprised her: desert country, after all! They drove past row upon row of simple plastic greenhouses, and then a hill crowded with pale gray cement-block houses; under the sunless gray sky, the pale gray houses looked like gravestones marching up the hill. But it was the center of Amman that surprised her even more: tall office buildings stood next to vacant lots filled with piles of cement blocks and idle bulldozers, followed by grand villas and opulent houses. But there was so much building that it was like a vast downtown being taken apart and rebuilt, with many gaps of vacant land sandwiched between great new modern structures and everywhere the look of big money being spent.

"The city glitters," murmured Mrs. Pollifax.

Over his shoulder Joseph said, "Here, yes—this is central Amman, embassies, rich people's houses—rich Palestinians—but there are many refugee camps, too. Many, many!"

They turned down a narrow side street lined with shops and colorful awnings; men in denim work clothes, long gray robes, long beige robes; men seated on the sidewalk gossiping; a few children but no women. They were then back to a busy main thoroughfare, where they drove through the crescent-shaped entry to the hotel, and it was very grand indeed. Leaving his blinker lights on, Joseph carried out their luggage and escorted them into the lobby to the registration desk.

"I will leave you a few minutes while I park my car on the street," he told them. "But I will return to learn your plans, okay?" He smiled. "Over a cup of coffee, my treat."

Mrs. Pollifax said lightly, "That I will leave to you, Farrell; come see me, I prefer to unpack." Having registered, she held up her key for Farrell. "Room 308," she told him; a porter picked up her suitcase, and she was ushered to the elevator.

Once in room 308, after investigating bath, closets, and the view from her window, she brought her clothes out of her suitcase, shook out the wrinkles, and hung them in the closet. From her carry-on bag she removed toothbrush and toothpaste and delivered them to the bathroom. Returning to her carry-on bag she reached into it again and met with an unfamiliar object. She drew it out with a frown.

It was the plaque that Mr. Nayef had tried to sell her on the plane, the carving of the Urn Tomb at Petra.

Mrs. Pollifax looked at it with exasperation. Apparently Mr. Nayef had reconsidered his sales pitch, and because she had admired the plaque—however politely—he had very kindly slipped it into her carry-on bag while she was in the lavatory. But what a nuisance, she thought. Generous of him, but not at all what she'd select as a souvenir. She tossed it into the wastebasket and then, feeling guilty, extracted it and examined it with hostility. On close inspection she saw that it was the thick plywood mounting that degraded it; the carving itself was the work of a gifted miniaturist. It was possible that Cyrus might like it, being more interested in ancient history than she was, and certainly he would know who the Nabataeans were, who had long ago carved the Urn Tomb out of a rock wall.

Her box of writing paper was in the bottom of her carry-on bag. She dug it out and placed the plaque inside of it: a perfect fit, and then she removed one sheet of writing paper, sat down, and wrote, "Dear Cyrus, I've arrived at last, and—"

Hearing a knock on her door she slipped the sheet of paper back in the box on top of the plaque and opened the door to Farrell. "Greetings," she said, smiling. "What time is dinner?"

"At seven-thirty, Joseph tells me, and I've asked him to join us. We meet in the lobby. It's buffet, so you can pick and choose between American and Middle Eastern."

"Good," she said. "You had coffee with Joseph and made all the arrangements, I take it, but how on earth did you explain our spending all morning at Karak castle tomorrow, and possibly still another morning there?"

"Damned awkward, yes," admitted Farrell cheerfully. "I hope like hell Ibrahim shows up tomorrow, but I did prepare Joseph for the worst. He didn't question it—he's young and obviously wants to please."

"And just how did you prepare him?" she inquired suspiciously.

He grinned. "I think I was quite creative.

We now have an archaeologist friend finishing up his work in Syria—they do a lot of digging there—and we're not sure which day he'll get here—and I had no idea what hotel I'd find in Amman—and since our friend is terribly interested in seeing Karak castle—and our being crazy Americans—it was left that we'd meet at the castle.

"I am also," he added with a wicked grin, "paying Joseph a reckless amount of money for his showing us around his country. He dreams of acquiring a real tour bus, you see."

"Farrell! You're bribing him?"

He nodded. "Ruthless, that's me." He glanced at his watch. "Let's check out that shop in the lobby, I think I saw maps for sale there."

This idea Mrs. Pollifax embraced. "Because," she pointed out, "you gave me no time to learn exactly where we *are,* and I'd like to learn just how far Ibrahim must come to reach Jordan."

They descended in the elevator, and Farrell led her to the shop, where he found a map of Jordan, and Mrs. Pollifax, browsing, bought a map of Amman and a stamp for the letter to Cyrus she hoped to complete soon. In the lobby they pulled together two chairs and spread out the maps.

Again she was surprised at how small Jordan—the Hashemite Kingdom of Jordan—looked next to the huge country of Saudi Arabia that lined both its western and southern borders. "And there's Iraq," she said, pointing. "Oh dear, such a small, squeezed-in border *there.* Many guards, do you think?"

Farrell was frowning. "Carstairs thought Ibrahim might have to come by way of the desert—a killing route—since no visas are issued in Iraq and the borders are tight. Our friend might have to drop down into Saudi Arabia to find a relatively safe place to cross."

"How about Jordan's borders?"

Farrell hesitated. "There's a Desert Patrol. . . . I don't *think* the borders are fenced because I seem to remember there were treaties allowing the Bedouin in Jordan to still roam back and forth with their herds of sheep and camels. For the sake of pasturage." He added doubtfully, "But now that the government has persuaded many of the Bedouin to leave the desert for the villages, they drive pickup trucks instead of camels, and that leaves only the sheep." He shook his head. "I don't know."

"Joseph might."

Farrell laughed. "Try fitting *that* question into a casual conversation. Anyway, here's the Governate of Karak, see? And the town of Karak—" He glanced up. "And here comes Joseph."

Mrs. Pollifax nodded. "Looking very handsome and professional in a blazer with a Jidoor Tours insignia on its pocket."

Joseph gave them each his warm smile; to Mrs. Pollifax he said, "And did the man asking for you find you okay?"

Mrs. Pollifax stiffened. She was aware of Farrell, beside her, turning to give her an astonished glance. "A man?" she faltered. "Asking for *me*?"

"He did not find you? The room clerk is a friend of mine and said—"

Farrell interrupted to say sharply, "You're sure he wasn't asking for *me*?"

"No, no, for Mrs. Pollifax." He was beaming now, apparently pleased that she had a friend in his country. "If you had told me—"

Calmer now, Mrs. Pollifax said, "I can't think who it would be, Joseph. Perhaps you could ask your friend the room clerk if he is very *certain* it was a Mrs. Pollifax he asked for, because he must have mistaken the name. You'll do that?"

"Of course," said Joseph. "He is not on duty now, but when I see him again, yes."

"Because," pointed out Mrs. Pollifax, "I don't know anyone in Jordan."

Joseph gave her a startled glance but said nothing.

"So you see what a mystery it is," she told him, smiling. "Shall we go in for dinner now? I'm ravenous."

To Farrell she said, in a low voice, "Stop looking stunned, I can give you an endless list of names like mine."

"I don't believe it."

She said lightly, "Then I'll recite some of them for you, even if I've only met most of them in telephone directories: Polidore, Pollander, Pollard, Pollett, Polifroni, even Polystar. . . ."

She was relieved to see his face relax

into an amused smile. On the other hand, having cheered Farrell, she felt a sudden and oppressive sense of unease that she couldn't explain, but which seemed to be lurking in her subconscious, not quite reachable.

They met again at breakfast, where Mrs. Pollifax discovered Middle Eastern yogurt, thick and textured and tart. "Now this is *real* yogurt," she told Farrell, ladling it over her cornflakes until it lay there like a blanket.

Farrell made a face. "Thanks, I prefer bacon and eggs."

"No sense of adventure," she told him with a twinkle.

"Ha," snorted Farrell, and with a critical glance at her, "Why on earth are you hunched forward like that in your chair?"

"Knapsack," she said.

"Knapsack? Why don't you take it off, for Pete's sake?"

"Because," she said bitterly, "I'll never get it on again, I've absolutely no logic about the straps. Cyrus gave it to me for my birthday, he has his own for bird-watching. It took me ten minutes in my room to figure out how to put it on backward."

"You mean on your back," he said, amused. "What are you carrying in it, if I may ask?"

"A sweater, an extra pair of shoes, writing paper to finish a letter to Cyrus while we wait at the castle, and a head scarf. It frees the hands," she pointed out, and changed the subject by asking, "If Ibrahim doesn't show up this morning, how many mornings do you propose visiting the castle?"

He shrugged. "Antun urged three mornings and left it up to me what I do after that, but he reminded me that I'd have to confront the fact that Ibrahim could be caught somewhere along the way, sent to prison, shot, or dead in the desert."

Mrs. Pollifax sighed. "I can understand why the manuscript couldn't be mailed, but surely somewhere, somehow in Iraq—?"

"We no longer have an embassy or consulate there, Duchess, not since the Gulf War. The Polish Embassy handles our complaints, and even the most innocent people who wander across the Iraq border are clapped into prison, suspected of being spies."

Mrs. Pollifax shivered. "Such madness! I wonder . . . can one man's book make a difference? Is it worth Ibrahim's risking his life?"

Farrell smiled. "When I visited Antun Mahmoud the night before I telephoned you, I asked him the same question. He quoted to me an Arabic saying—and I sure hope I get it right." He closed his eyes, remembering, and said softly, " 'The words of eloquent men are like a mighty army, and their writings like glittering swords.' "

" 'Like glittering swords,' " she repeated. "Yes, I like that."

Further conversation was interrupted by Joseph's arrival, and he was filled with enthusiasm. "You are ready to leave? I want you to know everything about Karak castle," he said, handing them each several sheets of mimeographed paper. "My car is parked on the street," he added. "Shall we go?"

They followed him out of the hotel, threading their way past a dozen tour buses lined up and waiting. "You must understand," he said, as they walked toward his car, "this castle is very old, fourteenth century. It rises so high, and is built of such massive blocks of stone, that building it was an amazing feat in those times. But of course," he added, "whoever controlled the castle controlled the land. It was fought over many times. And *brutally.*"

"Who wanted it?" asked Farrell, as they climbed into the car.

Joseph laughed. "Everyone! For instance, it took Saladin—you have surely heard of Saladin—it took him eight months to capture it. It was of big importance to the caravan route that came through the mountains to Damascus."

He received no response, and Mrs. Pollifax felt sorry for him, but it was scarcely eight o'clock and she had not realized that Amman was half a mile above sea level, and the combination of jet lag and change of altitude promoted a strange lassitude. She thought ruefully, *I should have had that second cup of coffee, this may be the morning we meet Ibrahim.* This brought a flare of excitement that banished her drowsiness; she sat up straight and turned her attention to the road.

At eight in the morning the traffic was heavy until they left the center of Amman behind, heading south on a highway filled with roadside signs: ARAB EXPRESS, IRAQI-JORDAN TRANSPORT COMPANY, COCA-COLA, VOLVO, TOYOTA, DATSUN. . . . This district was one of estates, lavish forty-million-dollar homes. Joseph said, "rich Palestinians," and then they left behind the outskirts of the city to drive through an endless plain of gravel, until the road headed upward toward the hills, past groves of pine trees—"green at last," said Mrs. Pollifax, "and greenhouses again—so many!" Here the surrounding country-side held folds and hollows in which herds of sheep grazed, and she counted fig trees and pomegranates in the gardens, and olive and apricot trees planted in ser-ried rows.

They passed a village with its square white houses and minarets washed in the gold of the morning sun, surrounded by terraced gardens and flat rock walls. Jo-seph slowed his car, and they looked down into a valley with a breathtaking view of tawny hills, one after the other, until they vanished into a misty horizon.

"Jordan Valley," said Joseph. "At night, from here, you can see the lights of Jerusalem."

Even Farrell was now wide awake.

The road that followed gave the appearance of being carved out of the rocky mountainside, and Mrs. Pollifax noticed small caves carved out of the stone, and then they drew up to a checkpoint.

A soldier in an olive green uniform walked out of his kiosk to approach them. He hailed Joseph by name, apparently knowing him; they exchanged words and Joseph drove on.

Mrs. Pollifax said in surprise, "Your cars and trucks don't have horns! Just a sort of *click-click,* like a snapper or a tongue clucking."

Joseph laughed. "We are polite, you see, and we are a small country. A friend of mine visited New York City and—what is your expression, wow? He was sure he would come home deaf."

"I don't wonder," Farrell said.

"Speaking of politeness," began Mrs.

Pollifax, "would it be very rude of me, Farrell, to ask whether you and Kate Rossiter are still seeing each other? When the two of you left Sicily together—"

He interrupted to say flippantly, "We are—to use the vernacular—just friends now, another way of saying we exchange Christmas and birthday cards, no more."

"I'm sorry," she said. "Are you angry about how it turned out?"

He shrugged. "You know how it is—or was. She loves doing fieldwork, and apparently loves the danger of it. Very stimulating, she calls it! Me, I was active in the CIA for what feels now an eternity, and I had to bow out. Too *much* stimulation, living a double life. Call it burnout. We simply met at the wrong time."

Mrs. Pollifax nodded. She had respected Farrell's need for a change; he would always be available for a challenge—his working with freedom fighters in Africa had proved that—but from what she knew of his previous work for Carstairs, he was certainly lucky to be still alive, and for this she was glad.

"I'm sorry," she told him. "Do you know where she is now?"

He only shrugged. "Somewhere *stimulating,* no doubt, gathering information under a false name. Guatemala or Algeria or Russia or Bulgaria, you name it."

Mrs. Pollifax said no more.

It was nine o'clock when they reached the busy little town of Karak, passing a marketplace that left a kaleidoscopic impression of rubber tires for sale, children's bicycles, burlap sacks of grain, and sides of meat. Then they were in the countryside again, the castle looming huge in the distance, rising tier by tier out of its bed of rock, an incredible, half-ruined bastion.

"There is a museum here, but it is closed today," said Joseph, as they parked in the shade. "It's early, no tour buses yet. What time do you expect your friend, Mr. Farrell?"

Farrell and Mrs. Pollifax exchanged glances. He said casually, "No specific time, Joseph, just at some point during the morning. As I mentioned before, it's uncertain *which* day, and we may have to come tomorrow, too."

Joseph nodded, but his glance at Farrell was puzzled. "Yes, of course," he murmured. "I see."

Mrs. Pollifax hoped that he did not see too *much* and, once out of the car, quickly changed the subject by asking, "What's that you're carrying, more information for us?"

"This?" he said. "Oh—oh yes, I thought you might be interested. Pictures of how the men dressed. Photocopied," he added self-consciously, "from a book in the university library."

He really is a conscientious guide, she thought, and held out her hand; he distributed pages to each of them, and they leaned against the car to look at them. "Good heavens," said Mrs. Pollifax, her glance sliding from pictures of men in armor to the words below. "This requires a new vocabulary! 'Man number two is in articulated steel plates over gambeson and habergeon, with steel-plated helmet called an armet'?"

Farrell grinned. "I'm looking at 'metal leg and arm defences over habergeon,'" he contributed, "'with shorted jupon and plate gauntlets and rowel spurs.'"

Suddenly mischievous, Joseph confided that his favorite was the fifteenth-century sallet and bevor. "I will show you them in the museum in Amman this afternoon, but I thought—thought you might like to imagine them *here.*"

Mrs. Pollifax nodded. "One can imagine that, yes."

He led them toward the castle. "We enter here, through this narrow opening, and first you see the stables for the war-horses. We go down—watch your step!"

It was dark, like walking into a silent tomb, with a smell of dust and age and chill. "Let's keep it short," Farrell said firmly. "I doubt my friend—if he comes—will look for me in the stables."

They walked over uneven ground down a line of low-ceilinged stalls, and then Joseph led them up worn stone stairs, where they had to grasp each others' hands to keep from stumbling in the darkness. They peered into small earth-floored rooms with only tiny slits of light to illuminate them; they climbed up and down steps, and then into a large earth-floored hall.

"With a hole in the center through which," pointed out Joseph, "well—it is a toilet hole," he explained with a frank smile.

At last he brought them out into daylight, on a perilous shelf of stone lacking any walls. "Here," he said, "is where prisoners were thrown over the side and down into the moat to their deaths."

Mrs. Pollifax winced; drawing as near to the edge as she dared, she looked down, and it was a long way down. "How horrible!"

Farrell, looking a little sick, said, "Surely there's a pleasanter place to view the landscape and watch for my friend."

Joseph smiled. "Of course, and I take you there."

"Much better," said Mrs. Pollifax, as they reached an outside gallery with the security of low walls, and saw far below a panorama of brown hills threaded with roads and small patches of green. From here they could look down on the parking area and the entrance below; the sun was bright, and a refreshing breeze ruffled her hair. "A good place to spend the morning," she acknowledged, looking from earth to sky, and then she turned and looked back and up at the walls above,

with their tiny slits for windows. She found
it difficult to imagine people cooking,
sleeping, and living in such a cheerless,
dark, and tomblike castle. *But they would
be safe,* she thought. There would be that,
at least, with an army of men—in their
gambesons and habergeons, she added
humorously—ready to mount their war-
horses and ride out to fight their battles.

"Are we the only ones here?" she
asked, daring to lean over the low wall
and look down on Joseph's car.

"Early," Farrell pointed out, and removed a sketchbook and pen from his
pocket.

Mrs. Pollifax shrugged off her knapsack
and from it removed her sweater; Joseph
rushed to help her put it on, and she realized what a dull morning this was going to
be for him. Unless, of course, Ibrahim arrived very soon. She thought of the writing
paper she'd brought so that she could at
last write her letter to Cyrus, but she was
not only moved by Joseph's predicament,
she'd also decided that learning about
Jordan was of more interest to her just
now.

"Where did you go to university?" she

asked him, seating herself on the sun-warmed stone floor of the gallery.

"The Jordan University in Amman," he said, seating himself beside her with a smile. "When my family left the desert—"

"Left what?"

He nodded. "The desert. We are *bedu.*" Seeing her look blank, he added gently, "Bedouin . . . My grandfather, for instance, still lives in a tent. Not for him the city!" He shrugged. "He visits it but can't sleep in a house, so we visit him in the desert. It's good for us."

"I suppose it is," she said, alert now. "Your father—*he* left?"

"My father is a rug merchant, he sells Bedouin rugs in the souk. There is no polite education in the desert, you see—"

"Polite?" she echoed, smiling.

He laughed. "Did I use the wrong word? There is a great deal to learn from the desert—my sister Hanan is proof of that!—but my father wanted his children to be educated. In polite—no, proper schools." He added proudly, "I have one brother in the army, one brother in the police, a sister who teaches, there is myself—and then there is Hanan," he added with a grin.

"Hanan?"

"My little sister." His grin deepened. "She wishes to know if you have visited the Wild West and seen something called a road-o."

"Rodeo?"

"Yes." He laughed. "Hanan dreams of having a horse. She is eleven years old—she came so late!—and she is pure *bedu,* a wild one. You Americans have a word for it—tomcat?"

"Tomboy," said Mrs. Pollifax, with a smile.

"Thank you, yes. She is the delight of my grandfather and just as fierce and stubborn as he is. She loves the desert and goes there every chance she can. I do not think any man will tame her except someone like my grandfather, for she is just as strong-willed as he, and he says of her—my grandfather—'*Wellahi hadha, beduwi!*' "

"Meaning?"

He laughed. "It means, 'By my God, this one is a Bedouin!' "

"How unusual," murmured Mrs. Pollifax, and to Farrell, half seated on the wall and sketching, "I think we should invite Joseph and his sister Hanan to dinner at the hotel tonight; I'd like to meet her."

"So she can ask if you've seen a rodeo?" quipped Farrell. "I've been listening and wouldn't mind meeting her myself." He turned toward them with a frown. "But I thought women and children in the Middle East were—well, cloistered. Kept at home. They used to be, didn't they?"

"Oh yes," Joseph agreed, "but the war in 1979 changed much, you see. The men left to fight, and the women were needed in the police and the army. Some are in the police force still, but you will see some women veiled. The fundamentalists are very strict, but we—we are *bedu*."

Mrs. Pollifax considered this. "It's true that in Amman I've seen only one or two women in veils."

"In the villages you will see women in very heavy veils, called *burqa*." Joseph sighed. "We are such a small country, with a king who has survived many crises and many assassination attempts, and there are many, *many* more Palestinians in

Jordan now than Jordanians, and sometimes we fear—"

When he hesitated Farrell said, "Fear
what, Joseph?"

"I think it is our one big danger as a
country," he said quietly. "That the ex-
treme ones may become powerful and
force our women to wear the heavy veils
again and all of us to become unfree,
when we have become quite free here. Of
fear." He stopped, as voices were heard
from the interior, and a moment later a
guide appeared leading a dozen tourists.
Rising, he said, "I will bring from the car
the food I brought for you," and with a
glance at his watch, "If your friend does
not come I will show you this afternoon
the citadel and the museums."

Mrs. Pollifax nodded. "And you and
Hanan will join us for dinner?"

He bowed graciously. "We would be
honored."

4

There was no Ibrahim. Three tour buses came and went, but there was no solitary stranger looking for Farrell, and soon after noon they left, discouraged. They visited the citadel and two museums out of regard for Joseph, who assumed they were as interested as he was, and returned early to the hotel.

"A great deal of patience is going to be needed," Farrell said with a sigh as they shared the elevator to the third floor. "I confess I very much hoped he'd be there."

Mrs. Pollifax said philosophically, "At least we should go home with rather nice tans from so much sun at the castle. And tomorrow afternoon we visit Petra. Do we visit Petra even if Ibrahim comes?"

"We play everything by ear, Duchess. Have to. Going to nap, or shop, until dinner with Joseph and his sister?"

Mrs. Pollifax laughed. "No . . . *finally* I shall write Cyrus." Fumbling in her purse for the key to 308, she opened the door as Farrell continued down the hall to room 310. A moment later Mrs. Pollifax gasped, "Farrell!"

He turned. "What is it?"

"My room's been searched!"

"Nonsense," he said, joining her in the doorway. "Why on earth would—" and then, "Good God!"

Together they stared at the contents of her suitcase spilled out on the floor, her carry-on bag turned upside down on the bed and emptied. Farrell said in a dazed voice, "Damn clumsy job!"

"Very *rushed* job," she agreed.

"But out of all the rooms, why yours, and in a hotel like this one! Who would do this? Is anything missing?"

"Nothing at all," replied Mrs. Pollifax, after a glance at her clothes scattered across the floor.

"There might be some reason for *my* room being searched," said Farrell, looking baffled. "That is, if someone—heaven forbid—knows why I'm here, but why *your* room?" Seeing her face, he said, "Duchess, what's the matter?"

She had abruptly sat down on the bed, looking stunned. She said in a shaken voice, "Oh Farrell."

"Oh Farrell, *what*?" he demanded. "Don't look like that, you scare me, are you sick?"

"Farrell, there *is* someone—*was* someone—who knows my name and that I'm in Amman."

"Of course—Cyrus. Also Carstairs."

She shook her head. "Neither of them would have asked for a Mrs. Pollifax last evening at the desk downstairs."

He said impatiently, "No, but you said—"

"I know what I said," she told him, "but this—" She gestured toward the spilled contents of her carry-on bag. "It's too ridiculous, and yet—yet I did tell him my name."

"Who?"

"Mr. Nayef."

Farrell sat down beside her on the bed.

"Take a deep breath and enlighten me, will you? Who is Mr. Nayef?"

"He sat next to me on the plane. He talked and talked to me—about Jordan, because he said he was Jordanian—except that he was getting off at Amsterdam. He introduced himself, and I introduced myself."

"And?"

"And he said his firm in Amsterdam makes curios to sell to tourists in Jordan. He wanted me to buy one, even showed me one from his attaché case, a carving of the Urn Tomb at Petra, and told me he'd be happy to sell it to me at a discount, but I firmly said no."

Farrell sighed. "I'm listening but I'm not following any of this."

"That," she said, "is because you haven't seen what I found in my carry-on bag last evening." She shrugged off the knapsack on her back, unzipped it, lifted out her box of writing paper, and handed him the plaque. "He must have slipped it into the bag while I was in the lavatory. When I unpacked yesterday I nearly threw it away. This is what he wanted to sell me. . . . I thought it was a gift."

"Hmmm," murmured Farrell. "Did he think you were traveling alone?"

She thought back to that conversation on the plane; it seemed a very long time ago. "He asked me if I was traveling with the tour that was making so much noise, do you remember them? I said no. . . ." She frowned. "Yes, and then he asked if I had friends in Jordan, and when I said no he said something about how brave we American women are, and how free."

"Innocent Tourist traveling alone . . . Good God, Duchess, what did you get yourself into? All very well to think it a gift, but it sounds more likely he planted something on you. The oldest trick in the book."

"But what? And how?" she asked. "Drugs? Diamonds? It's just a plaque, it's only seven inches long, and how can any-thing—"

Scowling, Farrell interrupted her. "Let's first get everything straight, Duchess. He talked for an hour or two, you had dinner side by side, and then you went off to the lavatory, leaving your carry-on bag be-hind?"

She nodded. "Yes, after taking out the

smaller bag that held only what I'd need for the night. Toothpaste, cold cream, washcloth, toothbrush . . ."

"You were gone long enough for him to do this?"

She said ruefully, "It wouldn't have taken more than a minute, he need only have leaned over and down, unzipped my bag and quickly shoved the plaque to the bottom, zipped it up again, and put on his earphones to hear the movie." She added bitterly, "And he got off the plane at Amsterdam."

"Yes," pointed out Farrell, "giving him plenty of time—hours!—to fax or telephone to Amman, giving someone your description and your name, after which that 'someone' tried every three- and four-star hotel in the city to learn where you were staying."

She said dryly, "Whoever they are, they must be surprised to discover that I'm not traveling alone after all."

Farrell nodded. "Which—unfortunately—brings me into the picture, too. Let's look at this, Duchess, I mean really look at it."

She handed him the plaque, and he

carried it to the window. "Rather nice carving," he said, "but somehow it looks cheap as hell."

She nodded. "Because it's mounted on that cheap unvarnished plywood."

"The plywood, yes . . . which I'd guess to be at least three-quarters of an inch thick." Holding it closer to the light, "Now this is suspicious, Duchess, come and see. There's a thin line, barely visible, but I do believe we have two rectangles of plywood glued together."

She said tartly, "Then it's high time we learn what I smuggled through customs into Jordan. Have you a penknife, or do we bash this against the wall and split it open?"

"I've a penknife on my key chain," he told her. Reaching into his pocket, he brought it out and carefully inserted the tip into the line on the wood at one end, then at the other, and finally attacked the center. "Glued only around the edges," he said, and as he pried apart the two layers, they stared at what lay inside. "At least not diamonds or drugs," he said.

The center had been hollowed out just enough to conceal a key wrapped in tis-

suelike paper. Handing Mrs. Pollifax the
key he held the paper to the light, and
they both examined it.

"Arabic," she pointed out. "The words,
at least. The lines form a diagram, or is it a
map?"

"It's certainly no grocery list, Duchess,
but heaven only knows what it is."

"Heaven and Mr. Nayef, who obviously
wants it *back*," lamented Mrs. Pollifax,
and added with a sigh, "I should have
traveled in those bag lady clothes, he'd
never have dared to play such a trick on
me." She thought about this, frowning.
"Does it occur to you, Farrell, that customs would never have found this plaque
suspicious? I'm thinking it had to be Mr.
Nayef himself who didn't dare go through
customs."

"Persona non grata, you mean?" Farrell
made a face. "So what do we do with this
diagram and key? We sure as hell don't
need complications on this trip, Duchess."

With an ironic smile, she said, "I think
we already have complications, Farrell. If
this is why my room was searched, it's
only by the purest coincidence that I

tucked the box of writing paper and the plaque into my knapsack this morning. Do you think they'll give up finding it now?"

"I wouldn't bet on it," he said dryly. "I just wish we could get the Arabic words on this diagram translated so we know what the devil we've got on our hands."

"Ask Joseph?"

Farrell gave her a reproachful glance. "When we know nothing of him, or he of us? Unfortunately the logical thing to do would be to turn it all over to the police, but I have the strange feeling we'd never get to Karak castle on time tomorrow—we'd have to go through channels ad nauseam—and my top priority is Ibrahim, remember?"

"You're right, of course," agreed Mrs. Pollifax, with a sigh. "In the meantime, I'm wearing Cyrus's money belt, so why don't I tuck the key and diagram in with my traveler's checks?"

Farrell nodded. "Good idea, at least for the moment."

"So what is our plan of action now?"

"What we do first," said Farrell sternly, "is trade rooms. If they managed to get into this room once, they can do it again, and I insist you move into 310; number 308 is no longer impregnable."

"Farrell," she began in protest.

"I insist," he said. "Pack up your suitcase, I'll bring your knapsack and carry-on. Joseph and his sister must be waiting for us in the lobby by now, and we don't want to keep them waiting."

Reluctantly, Mrs. Pollifax crammed her clothes into her suitcase and carried it next door to room 310. Farrell, behind her, gathered up his own gear; they exchanged keys, and after leaving Farrell's suitcase in 308 they headed for the elevator, the dissected Urn Tomb under the pillow in room 308, and the mysterious key and diagram secure in the money belt Mrs. Pollifax wore around her waist.

5

Already Mrs. Pollifax had begun to regret so rashly inviting Joseph and his sister Hanan to join them for dinner. The events of the past hour had been unsettling; she would have liked to find the manager of the hotel and complain indignantly about her room being entered, but since nothing had been stolen it would only make her conspicuous. She was furious at Mr. Nayef, too, who had flagrantly used her, so that she could foresee becoming a burden to Farrell, who had enlisted her only as his "cover," as he put it, and certainly without expecting the intrusion of a Mr. Nayef.

Her spirits lifted, however, when she saw Joseph and his sister waiting for them in the lobby. Her spirits had a long way to rise, but it was a relief to see a new distraction far more pleasant than a burglary, and this was Hanan.

Joseph's sister Hanan, age eleven, stood very straight and small beside him, and not at all self-conscious among the well-dressed tourists. She wore a traditional long and shapeless brown dress, quite drab, enlivened by a huge white chiffon kerchief draped around her shoulders, but instead of the usual sandals— and Mrs. Pollifax did a double take at this—she wore a magnificent pair of white cowboy boots emblazoned with red stars. Her hair was cut short, with tight black curls like a cap framing a childish round face. Bright dark eyes searched the faces of everyone who emerged from the elevator, and when her brother pointed out Mrs. Pollifax and Farrell, she smiled eagerly, her teeth very white against her tan skin. Mrs. Pollifax found herself scrutinized with a keenness that she did not expect from an eleven-year-old child, but later she would learn that Hanan judged camels with just that intense and careful scrutiny.

"This is Hanan," said Joseph unnecessarily.

"How do you do, please," Hanan said gravely, shaking hands with each of them, and then, confidingly, "Did you know they sell maps in the shop here?" She held up two. "Of Amman and of Jordan—and the *desert.*"

Farrell said, "You don't have maps in school?"

"Oh yes, but nobody can take school maps home, these are *mine,*" she emphasized, hugging them with ardor.

"I'm wondering how you learned such excellent English," said Farrell.

Hanan beamed at him. "My grandfather learned it when the English were here— with Pasha Glubb—and my father and mother speak it—Youseff best of all—and we began studying it in fifth grade last year."

"Amazing," commented Mrs. Pollifax. "But let's continue this in the dining room, I hope you're as hungry as I am."

They proceeded to the dining hall, where Hanan's eyes widened as they passed the long line of buffet tables, with their silver tureens and exquisitely arranged platters of food. *"Hilweh!"* she murmured. "So *beautiful.*"

It proved a very interesting dining hour. Even before the waiter arrived to inquire if they wished bottled water, Hanan's maps were spread out across the tablecloth and the cutlery, nearly upsetting a vase of flowers. Farrell found himself explaining longitude and latitude, and Hanan was enchanted to learn that, in southwest Asia, Jordan was located at 29°11′–33°22′ north and 34°59′–39°18′ east—she liked numbers. She insisted on pinpointing precisely where her grandfather was camped during this month of *tishreen al-awal*— October—and wanted them to know that she possessed a camel of her own that was pure white.

"In Amman?" teased Farrell.

"In Amman?" She eyed him appraisingly. "My camel is with my grandfather in the desert." To Mrs. Pollifax, she added eagerly, "Please, I would like you to see my camel. Of course I wish for a horse, but not yet, my grandfather says."

"You're wearing cowboy boots," Mrs. Pollifax reminded her.

She nodded. "My grandfather had

them made for me in the souk. For *me,*" she emphasized.

"Yes," agreed Mrs. Pollifax. "That's very important, isn't it. That they're *yours.*"

It was established that neither Farrell nor Mrs. Pollifax had personally visited a rodeo, but this was forgiven by their young guest. Once the maps were folded up, they moved on to the buffet tables to choose from the lavish display of foods. Mrs. Pollifax, returning to their table with Joseph, said, "What will happen to Hanan, to such an independent child, Joseph? She's very unusual. I had thought that girls in your society were never allowed to be alone with a man, for instance, yet—"

"But she is not alone, I am her brother," he said, and then, with a sigh, "She came late to our family, you know. I am twelve years older, for instance, and she has had much more attention and free-ness. Yet I do not think she will grow up to teach, like my sister, or work in an office. I think she may probably marry her cousin Qasim; she amuses him, and Hanan admires his horses. He is sixteen and soon, I think, he may join the *badiya,* the Desert Patrol, because just like Hanan he says the city suffocates him, he needs the space of the desert and the sky."

"I would like to see that desert," she said. "Is it sand and dunes?"

Joseph laughed. "In places, yes, but in the deep desert, the Suwwan, it is all—what is your English word, flint stone? No, never much sand. Stones, gravel . . ."

"And space and sky," she said, nodding.

"Yes."

Hanan returned with Farrell, her plate full of desserts: pastries, cakes with candied frosting, and two cherry tarts with whipped cream; she ate contentedly while Farrell and Joseph planned their next day's ventures, beginning, of course, at Karak castle.

"But if you remain long at the castle," pointed out Joseph, "you will not have much time to see Petra. Which is special, you know, and important that you see. Unless you stay overnight near Petra? There is a good hotel, the Yaybat Zaman Hotel, at Wadi Musa."

"But it depends," interrupted Mrs. Pollifax. "If we meet Ibrahim tomorrow? If he comes?"

Farrell nodded.

"Perhaps he would like to see Petra, too," suggested Joseph politely. "I would charge no more for three people."

They exchanged glances but said nothing, and there was silence until Hanan said, "If you drive south tomorrow, Youseff, you could leave me at al Qātrāna."

"This is only Monday. *School* tomorrow," Joseph told her sternly. "Friday is no school. Maybe Friday."

"But Youseff, you know Awad Ibn Jazi has promised—"

She finished in Arabic, but Joseph was adamant. "*School,*" he repeated.

"And who is Awad?" asked Farrell, smiling.

"He was once a police officer in the Desert Patrol, the *badiya,*" explained Joseph.

Hanan nodded. "And he has promised to show me an old, old fort in the desert, half buried now, that only the *badiya* know about. Awad knows *everything*—how the smugglers come in from the border and where the hawks nest. He is older even than my grandfather—but he has no camels," she added regretfully.

"Hanan," Joseph said firmly, "if you have finished eating, we must go. You have school tomorrow, and our new friends have much else to do."

Unfortunately, thought Mrs. Pollifax, *too much to think about as well.*

Hanan at once rose from her chair. "*Ashkurak,*" she told them. "Thank you." And, shyly, "I like you very, very much, you will come and see my camel?"

"If we can," Farrell told her.

"We'll certainly try," promised Mrs. Pollifax.

"It has been a privilege," Joseph said, beaming at them, and politely bowed. "We thank you. Tomorrow morning at eight o'clock we meet again?"

They assured him they would be ready at eight o'clock, but as they lingered over their coffee, neither of them spoke; Mrs. Pollifax guessed that Farrell, too, was wondering what might have happened by tomorrow at this hour.

6

Bishop arrived at work that Wednesday morning to find Carstairs visibly upset and swearing softly under his breath. Seeing Bishop in the doorway he growled, "You might as well come in and let me vent my spleen on you."

Bishop closed the door behind him, sat down next to Carstairs's desk, and said cheerfully, "Be my guest. What's happened *now*?"

"What's happened now," said Carstairs testily, "is that I've just had a call from John Stover at the FBI, and—as you may have noticed—I'm furious. Possibly he is, too, but he's better mannered."

"So what's happened?" asked Bishop patiently.

"They learned yesterday—from an informer, mind you!—that Suhair Slaman managed somehow to slip through passport control and customs and spend three days in the United States. A terrorist like Slaman could have blown up who knows what in three days!"

Bishop winced. "How on earth did that happen? He's on every list, and his photograph posted at all the airports."

Carstairs said bitterly, "He came without his usual beard, as well as under another name, and obviously with an exquisitely forged passport."

"They've learned that much already?"

Carstairs nodded. "The FBI's had their sketch artist draw Slaman sans his beard, and the print is being circulated—too late, of course, damn it. They believe he flew *out* of Kennedy on the eighth."

"Two days ago," murmured Bishop. "Bound for where, and on what airline?"

"No idea yet, but they've found a security guard at Kennedy who recalls the face; he studies passengers who come through security pretty thoroughly. He thinks it was the eighth."

"But no idea what name he traveled under?"

Carstairs sighed. "No, but they're combing the passenger lists of the airlines, beginning with the Middle East flights, and showing the new sketch to all the stewardesses. Unfortunately, like birds on the wing, they have to wait for said flight attendants to come back on their return flights, so it's going to take some time. My own instinct is to begin looking for what mayhem he left behind him. Obviously something discreet, or we'd have read of it in the headlines."

"He may have been simply a courier," pointed out Bishop. "Delivering or collecting money."

Carstairs didn't bother to comment on this; any man with Slaman's penchant for murder would never tolerate being reduced to the status of courier. He said instead, "It had to be of some importance, whatever brought him here. There are extremists who rigidly live by the book and remain harmless, there are angry extremists who join groups and who simply protest, parade, and heckle, and then there are the Suhair Slamans, so full of hate they have to kill at the first signs of stability anywhere. Destroy, murder, undermine, upset . . . and clever, damn them."

"Didn't he use to live in Jordan?"

"Yes, but he'd never dare to set foot there again." He was silent a moment, and then he nodded. "If Suhair Slaman was in the country for three days and left on the eighth, then he would have flown into New York on October 4 or 5. I want newspapers, Bishop . . . New York, Chicago, Washington, Los Angeles . . . covering those three or four days. I doubt they've been microfilmed downstairs yet, so you'll need a cart. Let's see if anything surfaces."

Bishop said doubtfully, "You really think—"

"I don't think anything," Carstairs told him, "but a man like Slaman does *not* fly to the United States without some sort of mischief in mind. If it was to confer with someone, then we're out of luck. If it was to do what he does best—assassinate— there could be a report in the obituary columns, or in the news, however small."

"It's a long shot."

Carstairs said wryly, "Isn't everything?"

Bishop grinned and left, not too inspired by the thought of checking out four or five big-city newspapers when there were more important jobs waiting for him on his desk. When he returned he was even less sanguine because the time period included Sunday editions, triple in size.

Carstairs, however, was prepared to work with him, ignoring his own pressing work too, which surprised Bishop, but there was no reining in Carstairs when his curiosity was aroused. *Tangents,* thought Bishop, *forever going off on tangents.*

They set to work, beginning at the back of each newspaper, giving special attention to reports of any violence, as well as current obituaries. It was the October 8 *Washington Post* that brought an "Ah . . ." from Carstairs.

It was no more than eight lines of print under a modest heading of MUGGING ENDS IN DEATH. It had occurred in Washington on Massachusetts Avenue at eleven P.M., and it sounded like the typical robbery that had led to the victim resisting, and paying for this with his life. There had been no witnesses; cause of death was a knife slash to the throat. The report ended with the news that the man had been identified as Brahim Zayyad, who worked at the Jordanian embassy.

Carstairs read it again and frowned. "Interesting," he murmured.

"Do we stop work?"

"It's interesting, but we continue." Nevertheless Carstairs reached for a pair of scissors and neatly clipped the item out of the paper. "Let's see how many more news clippings we can add to this one."

But in the end there were no others, and Carstairs picked up the phone and put in a call to Detective-Lieutenant Gavin of the District of Columbia police.

"Carstairs here," he told him, when the connection was made. "I'm rather curious about the so-called mugging and death of a Jordanian embassy worker on the seventh."

Gavin's hesitation was interesting. "They've asked for as little publicity as possible," he said. "The deceased didn't work at the embassy, you see, he was a visitor. Member of the military—a colonel, actually—sent over to beef up security at the embassy, inspect and strengthen it.

He was due to return next week to Jordan."

"I see," said Carstairs. "Any idea what was stolen?"

"They admit only to a missing wallet."

"Think this was political?"

"Could have been," acknowledged Gavin. "It certainly upset them at the embassy. We were asked to treat it as a mugging, and for all we know that may have been what it was. Anything in this for us?"

Carstairs sighed. "Wish I could say yes, but for the moment I'm dealing only in hunches. Thanks, Gavin."

When he'd hung up Bishop said, "Do we give this hunch of yours to the FBI?"

Carstairs smiled. "You know what they think about my hunches. . . . Let's sit on it and see if they learn anything more about Suhair Slaman."

"You mean if Stover deigns to share it with us," said Bishop. "He doesn't have to."

Carstairs was optimistic. "He worked with us on the Bidwell case, and we handed that one to him. He owes us."

It was late afternoon when they heard

from Stover again. "Thought you'd like to know," he told them. "A Roberta Murshid, flight attendant on Royal Jordanian Airlines, has recognized our man Slaman from the beardless print. He sat in the last row of the plane on October 8—seat 42F—where the last-minute people usually end up. Fortunately he booked the flight himself and not through a travel agency, which simplified matters. The airline was very cooperative: the person occupying seat 42F was listed as a Mr. Nayef; he had a ticket to Amsterdam and would have left the plane there."

"Intriguing," said Carstairs. "Now I'll add what occurred to us after your call this morning," and he spoke of their discovery in *The Washington Post*'s October 8 edition.

Stover whistled through his teeth. "Another hunch of yours, Carstairs? He could have settled in Amsterdam for the moment; we'll have to see what we can turn up on a man named Nayef."

Carstairs hung up, looking thoughtful. "Amsterdam," he mused. "One has to wonder . . . for instance, if he was behind the mugging on Massachusetts Avenue, it strongly suggests that he's focusing on Jordan. He has connections in Syria—we know *that*—and Syria's next door to Jordan. He need only land in Amsterdam, hop on the next plane for Istanbul, and from there catch a direct flight to Damascus."

Bishop nodded. "Trouble?"

"What worries us—*most*," said Carstairs, frowning, "is too damn many people over there in Jordan who resent King Hussein signing the peace treaty with Israel. He's got powerful enemies in his Islamic opposition party who feel betrayed. It's a difficult time for him." He sighed and shook his head. "This definitely needs reporting at once to our office in Amman. Make a note of it, Bishop. As for us—"

"Yes?"

"As for us, it's time to get back again to today's work. Off with you!"

7

On their second morning at Karak castle Joseph cheerfully entertained them with stories of his grandfather, who had known the Englishman John Bagot Glubb who formed the Arab Legion that became the first Jordanian army. After this Joseph became very serious, very pedantic, as he visibly changed into his Lecturer role and described Petra, which they would visit in the afternoon. Mrs. Pollifax exchanged glances with Farrell and he winked at her, but he too rearranged his face, acquiring an expression of equal gravity as he listened. "What do you mean, Petra was 'lost'?" he asked.

"For hundreds of years no one knew it was there, no one remembered. Long, long ago it was a very busy caravan stop on the way to Damascus, the Spice Route that continued through the desert to Damascus and Aleppo. You will see why it was forgotten: a canyon, very deep and surrounded by mountains, hidden away with only one entrance, unless a person climbed one of the mountains and looked down on it. Only the Bedouin knew of it and camped there all those years, until an explorer named Burckhardt discovered it again in 1812."

"Is there still only one entrance?" asked Mrs. Pollifax.

"Oh yes. That is by way of the Siq, which is over a mile long, a narrow passage through the rocks, very winding and in places completely overhung by the walls on either side."

"Quite an adventure, Duchess," said Farrell.

"There was once a flood in the Siq," added Joseph solemnly, "and many people drowned. It is so narrow, you see, and the water swept down from the mountains—very tragic—but now the water is diverted and there is no danger of *that*."

"Reassuring," said Mrs. Pollifax dryly. She was watching a flock of birds drifting lazily on the wind; *Cyrus would know what they were,* she thought, and then they flew off to the south, disappearing.

In midmorning Joseph brought out slices of the flat round bread that Jordanians called *khobz* and a jar of the thick yogurt she so liked. He spread the yogurt across the bread, which he then rolled, tubelike, around the yogurt, and after presenting this to her he made one for Farrell and for himself. Mrs. Pollifax carried hers to the wall and looked down, seeing that three tour buses had arrived; they could soon count on groups of tourists wandering out onto their gallery. If yesterday was a sample, the three of them would be regarded with much curiosity while they listened to the guides speaking in Arabic, German, or English; at seeing them, the polite ones would appear almost apologetic at intruding on their privacy, while several people would want to see what Farrell was sketching, and it would all be quite tiresome.

Unfortunately only one passenger car arrived, a rusty red sedan, and although she and Farrell watched it with great hope, the two men inside did not get out, and after an interval the sedan drove away.

By 12:15 they knew there would be no Ibrahim on this second morning, either, and Mrs. Pollifax saw that Farrell was looking grim, and as they descended the narrow dark stairs and left the castle, he was oppressively silent, his brows drawn together. In silence they drove through the town of Karak, but when they reached the Desert Highway Mrs. Pollifax's attention was diverted by a rusty red sedan that pulled out of a dusty side road and fell in behind them. The same car, she realized, that had parked at the castle and then driven away, and the same dark outline of two men in the front seats. She wondered, with a flare of hope, if one of them could be Ibrahim, perhaps not sure of Farrell yet, or possibly unprepared to find him with a guide and a woman. Yet neither of the occupants of the car had entered the castle, she remembered, so how could they have inspected Farrell or known that he was accompanied by two people? Her glance moved to Joseph, and she saw that he was looking into his rearview mirror; their eyes met, and she understood that he too was noticing the car behind them as they drove south to Petra.

She did not turn to look again, nor did she nudge Farrell, but she remained aware of Joseph's frequent and interested glances into the mirror. She gave her attention instead to the countryside, with its fertile fields of rich brown earth and the many greenhouses lining the road, as well as signs advertising NABIL FOOD PRODUCTS, ARAB BANK, KUMHO TIRES, GOODYEAR, and FIRESTONE, and then the road turned upward and stony mountains lay ahead.

They wound their way down the road into Petra to meet with lines of parked tour buses, as well as a post office, a Tourist Police Station, a shop selling film and T-shirts, and a number of tourists mounting horses.

"Horses!" cried Mrs. Pollifax in horror.

Farrell grinned. "Didn't you know? Horses, yes. Or you can walk down the Siq—a long walk—"

"Or there are horse carts," emphasized Joseph.

Horse carts sounded cowardly, but Mrs. Pollifax admitted to feeling unnerved at the prospect of climbing on a horse.

She was remembering her experience in Albania on a donkey, and a runaway horse in China from which she'd been thrown, breaking her wrist.

Patiently Joseph explained that each horse was led on a rope by its owner, usually a Bedouin with family nearby.

"Led?" she faltered. "*Slowly?*"

"Slowly," he said firmly. "Come—I show you. Each horse is numbered. You like this one? This is number 24, and it will be this same horse number 24 that will meet you later down in the canyon, after you have seen Petra, and at whatever hour we choose."

She eyed with suspicion the man waiting stoically beside horse number 24, a black horse with a jolly red saddle blanket. The man looked experienced, if tired. He wore a white headscarf or *kaffiyeh,* secured by a black woven cord called an *aigal,* dull gray trousers and jacket. He had a scrawny mustache under a somewhat bulbous nose, a lined but patient dark face.

"And his name?" she asked. "He won't allow the horse to gallop?"

Joseph laughed. "His name is Mohammed, and since Mr. Farrell grows bored with sightseeing I will ask Mohammed to meet us with the number 24 horse down there—" He pointed in the direction of the Siq. "—in one hour. To bring us back here."

Allowing herself to be persuaded, Mrs. Pollifax mounted. The horse seemed extremely broad and very high, and as they moved ahead toward the dark cleft of the Siq she devoted herself entirely to not falling off, which felt only a matter of time because the horse swayed from side to side, with odd small lurches. As she and Mohammed entered the dim passageway Farrell passed her, waving, and then Joseph. High above she could glimpse a slit of blue sky framed by the towering rock walls; ahead the passage narrowed as it slanted downward. Behind her came the sudden clattering of hooves, and two local boys galloped past at high speed. *Show-offs,* she thought indignantly. As they continued, however, she began to catch the rhythm of the sways and various lurches of the horse and to feel almost swashbuckling, and just as the passage threatened to become claustrophobic, it widened, the slope leveled, and she saw sunshine ahead.

They emerged at last into Petra, the hidden city. And there, on her left, towered the famous treasury building pictured in Farrell's guidebook.

With difficulty Mrs. Pollifax dismounted, politely thanked Mohammed, and was joined by Farrell and Joseph. At once Joseph proceeded to enlarge upon the facts that he'd already given them. . . . The city had been inhabited by Nabataeans, Greeks, Romans . . . the camel caravans that had long ago passed through with their cargos of spices had often been plundered by the Nabataeans . . . the Queen of Sheba herself had passed this way, and traces of habitation had been found dating back to 10,000 B.C. . . . but what most interested Mrs. Pollifax was the fact that no building in the canyon of Petra was free-standing; all had been carved into the face of the sandstone cliffs. She stared in awe at the height of the *El Khazneh,* or treasury building, and tried to picture workmen risking their lives a hundred feet above the earth to carve ornamented columns out of solid rock.

How many had fallen to their deaths? If it was now a romantic corner of the world to visit, she doubted it was a romantic place to live thousands of years ago: there would have been plunder, wars, virulent diseases, bad plumbing, droughts, and floods. Yet obviously there was this great hunger for beauty: to honor their gods, to honor their ancestors, to assert and honor themselves, and all of this hidden away in the desert, a secret. Mrs. Pollifax enjoyed secrets, having experienced a hidden life of her own after beginning assignments for Carstairs about which—still—so few knew.

If there was an Urn Tomb they did not find it, but there was a sufficiency of tombs. Entire rock faces were pitted with entrances, which, after much climbing up and down, proved to be either burial chambers or caves where the Bedouin had once lived.

But Farrell, only a pseudo-sightseer, grew restless, and her number 24 horse and Mohammed were waiting, except that when they reached the mounting platform and a horse was led up for her, it was not Mohammed leading it but a young man in blue jeans with a red scarf tied around his head.

"But where's Mohammed?" she asked. "This can't be number 24!"

Joseph laughed. "Never mind, it's your horse, see? Number 24 definitely—all *bedu* have relatives!"

It was easy, mounting from a platform. Farrell and Joseph mounted behind her and rode ahead while she plodded along at a sedate pace, more confident now about riding as they entered the Siq and began the slow climb upward out of the canyon.

They had reached a point where the passage narrowed when the young man leading her horse stopped. The horse stopped, too, and Mrs. Pollifax, hoping he understood English, asked, "What is it?"

He turned and looked up at her, smiling. Dropping the lead rope he pointed, still smiling, and feeling rather cross, she said again, "What *is* it?"

He brought out a knife and, walking to her side without a word, reached up to her knapsack and prepared to calmly cut it free from her shoulders.

She stared down at him in astonishment, and then, "Stop that!" she cried angrily. Freeing a foot from its stirrup she kicked him; at once he dropped his knife and seizing her foot pulled her off the horse. She landed on her knees. With no regard for her as a human being he picked up his knife and resumed slicing away at the thick strap of her knapsack, his attention completely concentrated on removing it.

She stumbled to her feet. The Siq was empty of people: there was no clatter of hooves and no voices. Erect at last, Mrs. Pollifax braced herself, managed to step an inch or two away from him, and furiously delivered a quick and incisive karate chop to the young man's jaw. With a gasp he sank to the earth.

Mrs. Pollifax slung the knapsack over her arm, one strap dangling, and was now faced with the urgent problem of climbing back on the horse. She placed one foot in a stirrup, jumped, wrestled her way across the back of the horse, found the reins, and nudged the creature with her knees. He began walking, then broke into a gallop, and Mrs. Pollifax, badly placed and insecure, lost the reins, fell forward with both arms around the horse's neck, and in this manner raced out of the Siq, rather like a cork out of a bottle.

Farrell, waiting for her, said, "What on earth!" His eyes narrowed as he saw her flushed face and the knapsack hanging from her arm by one strap. Helping her off the horse, he said, "Duchess, what—?"

"Where's Joseph?"

"Walking toward us right now."

"Someone must have been bribed," she gasped. "Farrell, he had a knife. A knife, *and he wanted my knapsack.*"

Farrell's lips tightened. "The one item not in your hotel room when it was searched. Where is he now?"

"Still back in the Siq, probably regaining consciousness. Farrell—"

"No police," he said flatly. "Let's go. Go fast," and to Joseph, "We'd like to leave now, Joseph. Mrs. Pollifax's horse ran away with her and she's upset."

"Yes, of course," Joseph said, looking at her curiously, and they walked toward the car, Mrs. Pollifax limping a little from her fall. She climbed into the taxi with Farrell beside her and with the knapsack on her lap, and Joseph started the car.

As they left Petra behind them a dull red sedan appeared again, with only one man in it now, and devotedly followed them—at a distance—all the way back to Amman.

It was late when Joseph left them at the hotel, and while Farrell headed for the dining room, promising to keep it open for her, Mrs. Pollifax hurried upstairs to change into clean slacks and to rinse the dirt from the knees of those she'd worn at Petra.

When she entered the dining room fifteen minutes later she was surprised to see that Farrell was not alone. With him at his table was a man in a black silk suit, with dark hair and a mustache flecked with gray, talking eloquently with a flutter of hands to make a point. As she approached, Farrell rose; his companion looked startled, turned, and gave Mrs. Pollifax a glance that she interpreted as unwelcoming, or at least annoyed.

"My traveling companion," Farrell said, alluding to Mrs. Pollifax but not giving her name. "A second American for you to meet—before you return to your table."

A not-so-subtle hint, thought Mrs. Pollifax, wondering how long the man had been there, and she sat down in the third chair. Farrell had already visited the buffet and his plate was heaped with food: stuffed grape leaves, chicken, eggplant, and hummus. He said, "This is Mr.—"

"Names are so unimportant," the man said, with a smile.

"He has been instructing me," said Farrell, "in Islamic literature."

"How kind of you," responded Mrs. Pollifax.

The man nodded. "Yes, novels are fairly new to us Arabs, but we have some very fine novelists now. The women authors—" He shrugged. "—tend to write tragedies and whine about oppression, but we also have fine writers who propose an Islamic political system and ideology, such as in Egypt—" He named two authors.

"Rejecting the modern," said Farrell, nodding gravely.

"Rejecting all *Western* influences," he said, correcting him. "Quite unlike old-fashioned, European-tainted writers, such as—perhaps you are familiar with the work of Dib Assen?"

Mrs. Pollifax gave Farrell a quick glance, thinking this a somewhat strange coincidence.

Farrell repeated the name doubtfully. "I may have read something of his published in English, the name is vaguely familiar. He's an Iraqi, isn't he?" To Mrs. Pollifax he said, "But you've not visited the buffet yet!" Rising he added, "I'll go with you, I want to look over the desserts," and to the stranger, "Nice to have talked with you, I wish you a pleasant evening."

The man was being dismissed. He looked angry for a moment, and then smiled charmingly and rose. "I will leave you to your dinner. You two are related?"

"Cousins," said Mrs. Pollifax firmly, and as they approached the buffet, "And where did he come from? I thought it interesting, his mentioning Dib Assen."

"*Too* interesting," Farrell said. "He's watching us, by the way. He's with two other men; I can't tell whether they're watching us, too. I recommend the stuffed grape leaves, by the way." He looked troubled, and she hastily selected her entrée, while he chose a cake, and they returned to their table in the corner.

Farrell, as if aware of being watched, pasted a smile on his lips, but his voice was grim. "He simply came over and very cordially asked if I was American and if I was enjoying my visit here, and he sat down. He also managed to ask tactfully— one might say artfully—what brought me here. But his eyes didn't smile."

"Yours aren't smiling now," she pointed out.

"No. He hoped I had an excellent guide who was also able to tell me of the rich Islamic culture, above all Arabic literature, and if you don't mind skipping dessert I think we need to talk. There's something I'd better tell you—and tell *myself,* too."

This was mysterious. "Let's go now," she said, and recklessly slipped her stuffed grape leaves into her napkin, and then into her purse. "I'll finish my dinner upstairs."

They rose silently in the elevator and entered her room. "All right, what is it?" she asked.

He sat down on the edge of the bed. "Something Carstairs told me when I visited him and that I took very lightly. He was so bloody casual about it—it came out just as I was leaving his office, like a throwaway line. He said that *others* might be after Dib Assen's manuscript, too."

"Others? Why?"

"Because it might not *be* just a novel. Because, damn it, Carstairs said that Dib Assen had done some work for *him.* For Carstairs . . . For the CIA."

She, too, sat down on the bed and stared at him. "Good heavens, Farrell, why didn't you tell me this before?"

"Because I didn't believe it—or didn't *want* to," he said bitterly, "and may I be damned for that, too."

"But—why?" she faltered. "Why wouldn't you believe Carstairs?"

He said savagely, "Pure vanity. Dib Assen knew that I worked for Carstairs—we were that close. He'd known about me for years, yet he never confided in me, never told me he knew Carstairs. Obviously he never trusted me enough. And that *hurt.*"

She looked at his contorted face and said gently, "But Farrell, you didn't live in Iraq."

"I know." His face was in his hands. "I know, I *know.* At least what this chap in the dining room has done for me . . .

he's reminded me of what Carstairs told me, and what I tuned out. He's put me on alert. But it doesn't explain him or the attack on you at Petra."

"Or the dark red sedan following us," she pointed out.

"No," he said, lifting his head, "but for pete's sake let's tomorrow take that key and plaque to the police, turn it over to them, and let *them* worry about it."

"Agreed," she told him, and smiled. "Farrell, you're tired. I recommend a very hot shower, a room-service snack, and a good night's sleep because we leave for Karak castle again in the morning."

He sighed. "Yes, for the third time, damn it, and still no Ibrahim."

At this same hour, in a different section of the city, Joseph was saying to his brother in a troubled voice, "I need your advice, Mifleh."

They sat on the balcony of the Jidoor house, the street below them dark except for a dim light still shining in the fruit stall across the way; the remaining stores were closed and padlocked behind shutters of steel. It was quiet except for a murmur of voices from downstairs: their mother, father, sister, and the television news.

"*Shu hada?*" asked his brother.

Joseph scarcely knew how to begin: Mrs. Pollifax and Mr. Farrell were Americans and very kind, as well as interested in him as a person. He and Hanan had shared a wonderful dinner with them at the hotel, and he was sure that both were good and respectable people, but he had his reputation and his future to consider, and he was quite aware that for the past day the same rusty-looking red car seemed always behind them at a distance; he could see this from his rearview mirror, as well as the shape of the two men inside. Joseph was ambitious, his dream was to one day own a proper tour bus, with brochures to place in hotel lobbies and distribute among travel agents, all of them advertising Jidoor Tours. Mrs. Pollifax and Mr. Farrell would leave Jordan in a few days, but this was his country, and his home, and if there was trouble what would happen to him?

After a glance at his face, Mifleh rose, left, and returned with two warm beers

. . . imported Amstel beers, too. These his brother could afford because he was in the Public Security Force; he'd had a year of military training and had then attended the Royal Police Academy in Amman. Now he was in the Department of Criminal Investigation, still new and unseasoned but definitely a member of the metropolitan police.

"I hear you have two rich customers this week," Mifleh said.

Joseph said bluntly, "We are being followed, Mifleh. Today, by the same car."

His brother's eyes narrowed. "Followed? You are sure? A police car?"

"They're usually white, aren't they? That's what I want to know—do the police ever drive a rusty dark red sedan?"

Mifleh shook his head. "Not likely, Youseff, unless it's undercover police. But this is strange, I agree. Did you take note of the license number?"

Joseph shook his head. "Too far behind us—always."

"Do your two customers know they're being followed?"

Joseph considered this. "I don't know, Mifleh. Once in a while Mrs. Pollifax turns to look behind us—I see this—but it is usually when I have pointed out a mountain or a mosque to see. But there is something more, Mifleh. . . . We visited Petra today. You know how the horses are always led down into the Siq and back later. On our return I rode ahead with Mr. Farrell, we waited at the top, at the visitors bureau, and Mifleh—suddenly her horse galloped out of the Siq—*galloped,* with her hanging around his neck—and she was alone, no man leading the horse, her face very flushed and hair untidy. She and Mr. Farrell spoke together quickly when she dismounted, and then Mr. Farrell said sharply, 'Let's go, Joseph.' "

"And you left?"

Joseph nodded. "But there was one other thing I noticed as we got into my car. She had worn a small knapsack on her back—it is popular these days, you know. Now she was carrying the knapsack, and one of the straps had been cut. It looked like a knife had sliced it away."

Mifleh whistled softly through his teeth.

"And the dull red car followed us back to Amman, but with only one man in it, not two."

"I am glad you told me this," Mifleh said. "I understand none of this, but it is strange, I agree. I hear that Hanan had dinner at the hotel with this woman and liked her?"

Joseph nodded.

"Because of the dinner at the hotel?"

Joseph shook his head. "Oh no, really liked her, Mifleh. Hanan is eager on Friday to show Mrs. Pollifax her camel, if it can be arranged."

Mifleh grinned. "Then she must like her *very* much."

"Yes."

Mifleh considered this, and then said, with a rueful smile, "Strange as it may be, Youseff, I trust our little sister. Has Hanan ever been wrong about a camel, a horse, a person? You remember how overjoyed we were when our father brought home the man from Egypt who had ordered ten fine expensive rugs to be shipped to him? Only Hanan disliked him and distrusted him—and the man never paid for the rugs our father sent—never, and it cost him dearly."

"I remember," said Joseph.

Mifleh finished his beer and rose. "I will

ask questions about any of our cars following two Americans named Pollifax and
Farrell. I am glad you spoke of it." He
reached out and touched his arm. "I know
you want your tour bus, I'll do what I can."

With relief, Joseph nodded. "*Shukram,*
Mifleh. You can do this without them
knowing? I don't want to lose them,
Mifleh, Mr. Farrell is paying more than I
dreamed of asking, and they are both
kind. Not like the others."

"Trust me, brother," said Mifleh, and
Joseph was content.

8

The next morning they once again set out along the Desert Highway for Karak and its castle. Farrell's sketchbook was filling: tired of scenery, brown hills, rocks, and patches of green, he had begun sketching Joseph's men in their habergeons and gauntlets and spurs, not copying them, but drawing them in a procession mounted on warhorses with flags flying. *He is good, really good,* thought Mrs. Pollifax, the lines of his sketches fluid and spontaneous as he brought the medieval world back to life in pen and ink. She had already expressed the hope to Farrell that he would sign one and allow her to buy it from him; Cyrus, she thought, would be especially fascinated.

As they drove south she said in a low

voice to Farrell, "And what have you decided about the Man in the Black Silk Suit last evening?"

"I don't know," admitted Farrell. "There was an official air about him. . . . I would say that he was Someone, with a capital 'S.' "

"But how would anyone know about you?"

He sighed. "Only by searching Dib Assen's files and papers at his home in Baghdad. Only through knowing—or learning—that he once had a friend named John Sebastian Farrell. The other possibilities I prefer not to think about."

She nodded. "Torture, you mean. But if that was the case, then the Man in the Black Silk Suit would have to be—" She glanced at Joseph in front of them. "—have to be not Jordanian but from another country."

He nodded.

"And suddenly they find that a John Sebastian Farrell has arrived in Amman." She thought about this. "In fact they just may know more about *you* than about Ibrahim. Are we being followed?" she asked.

He turned and looked behind them. "Yes."

"Surely not by the Man in the Black Silk Suit," she told him. "Not after the attempt on my knapsack yesterday and my room being searched."

Farrell grinned. "You mean your friend Mr. Nayef."

She said bitterly, "Yes, with his advice on what to see in Jordan and his souvenir company in Amsterdam, blast him. We'd better be sure they follow us this afternoon to the police station in Amman so they'll stop all this nonsense."

They were silent for the remainder of the trip, thinking their own thoughts, each wildly hoping, too, that this third visit to the castle would produce Ibrahim at last. The only variety on the way was a long stop for dozens of sheep crossing the highway, with a shepherd in a long gray robe seated on a donkey overseeing their passage. The dull red sedan also stopped, but at a discreet distance, and once they passed through Karak and neared the castle the car disappeared, no doubt to wait for their departure and resume following them again.

A sleek black sedan was parked at the castle, and a tour bus had just arrived and was spilling out people in pairs. "We'll avoid them," Joseph said, after one long and envious glance at the bus. "The guide will lecture in each of the rooms, and—"

Farrell, his eyes on the sleek car next to the bus, interrupted him. "Good-looking Volvo. Someone else is here, let's look."

They entered into the darkness of the stables and toiled up steep narrow stairs, Joseph leading with his flashlight, and Mrs. Pollifax following with her pocket flash. Dust made her sneeze, and she was glad to see light ahead.

"A shortcut here," said Joseph, as they emerged on a long outdoor gallery.

"Fresh air at last!"

"Yes. We go down here, past these rooms to a staircase, quite hidden, and thus up to your favorite sketching place, Mr. Farrell."

"Good," said Farrell. "But tell me, just how was the castle captured by Saladin in 1189? By siege?"

Mrs. Pollifax smiled. Farrell's interest in the castle had been blossoming, whereas hers had begun diminishing after two long mornings here. Leaving them behind she walked ahead, stopping to peer into one of the rooms on her left, lit only by a slit in the wall, its earthen floor bare, and again she wondered who could have found such a tomblike space a home. Without venturing inside she proceeded toward the last room, more intrigued by the view from the parapet than by where she was going, when suddenly a man literally burst out of the room ahead, his face half-hidden by his loosened *kaffiyeh,* but his mouth discernible and open in a silent scream. He scarcely noticed her and she hugged the wall of the parapet to let him pass. It was as he raced past her that she saw the blood freshly smeared on the sleeve of his gray robe.

Without hesitation Mrs. Pollifax turned to the room he'd just left to see what had distorted that half-hidden face. The room was completely dark; Mrs. Pollifax turned on her tiny pocket flash and gasped as it shone on a man who lay sprawled on his back against the corner wall, empty eyes staring at the ceiling.

Desperately she called out, "Farrell! Joseph!"

At the panic in her voice, Farrell ran to her side. "Duchess, what—" Entering the room, he said, "Good God!"

She said in a shaken voice, "I think—think he's dead, Farrell. A man raced out of this room a minute ago, did you see him? With blood on his robe."

Joseph had followed them into the room with his more powerful flashlight. "*Bismallah,*" he gasped.

"Did *you* see him, the man who ran out?"

Farrell reached for Joseph's flashlight and said absently, "Someone passed us—we were talking."

Pointing, she faltered, "Can it be *Ibrahim?*"

"Hold the flashlight for me," Farrell told Joseph. "We've got to see if he's really dead." He leaned over the man, touching pulse and heart and nodded. "Unfortunately he's dead."

"Ibrahim?" repeated Mrs. Pollifax.

"I don't know—I'll have to search him." Farrell's voice was grim. "A man smuggling a manuscript, traveling with it, would package it and wear it strapped around his waist. At least, that's how I'd do it."

"But he's in Western clothes," pointed out Mrs. Pollifax. "And he's thin, he doesn't look at all padded."

"But how did he die?" asked Joseph. "Look, there's a dagger still in his hand, but I see no blood on *him.*"

Farrell was groping under the man's shirt, searching, baring his waist. "No manuscript," he said, sitting back on his heels and staring at the body.

"If not the man you were to meet," said Joseph, "who is he?"

With a sigh Farrell tucked the man's shirt back into his slacks and reached into the jacket. From an inside pocket he drew out a wallet. "It's in Arabic," he told Joseph, handing it to him. "This should tell us who he is."

Joseph stepped outside with Farrell following him. Mrs. Pollifax, curious, peered closer at the dead man, studying the angle of his fall, his head against the wall. Daringly she reached out and tipped his head forward to examine the back of it.

"Farrell," she called out, "the blood is on the back of his head, he had to have crashed against the wall. Joseph, let me have the flashlight, I see blood on his dagger, wet blood."

No one was listening. She rose and went out to join the other two, but one look at Joseph's stunned face silenced her.

"*What?*" demanded Farrell.

"He is Iraqi," Joseph said in a shocked voice. "And his address is First Circle, Jebel Amman—their embassy, and—" His face paled. "*Bismallah,*" he whispered, "he's *mukhabarat.*"

"What's that?"

"Secret police of the Ba'th party in Iraq. . . . Intelligence. Mr. Farrell, this is terrible—what have we met with?—we must call the police at once."

"I suppose so, yes," Farrell said reluctantly. "But how? Drive to Karak?"

"That tour bus may have a car phone. Some of them do. In case of breakdown."

"No," cried Mrs. Pollifax, "first we *must* find the other man. He was hurt, there was bright red blood on his sleeve and he—and he—"

"Could be Ibrahim," Farrell finished for her.

"Ibrahim?" repeated Joseph dazedly.

Impatiently Mrs. Pollifax said, "Please, there's no time for talk. Joseph, you know the castle, try to find the man; he's either hiding or on his way out. The exit needs to be watched, as well as that black car. I can do that from the top parapet where we've spent our mornings."

"You're right, of course," agreed Farrell. "I'll hunt down the tour guide and ask about a phone. Joseph—"

Joseph nodded. "I will need the flashlight again, please. Mrs. Pollifax, the stairs to the top of the castle—" He touched her arm and pointed, then raced down the gallery to begin his search.

Mrs. Pollifax, groping her way up another flight of dark stairs, was startled to find they led to a long dim room, which she vaguely remembered from Joseph's first-day tour. "Damn," she said aloud, furious that Joseph hadn't taken a few minutes to accompany her or to explain this aberration. In frustration she circled the room looking for a way out, sneezing from the dust stirred up by each footstep. Precious moments were wasted before she found the short flight of steps to the top of the castle. Hurrying to the edge of the parapet, she looked over the low wall and down. . . . The bus and the black car stood empty. A few minutes later she saw Farrell and the tour guide emerge from the castle and walk to the bus and enter it. Presumably Farrell had found a telephone.

No one else was in sight, except a woman and a boy walking down the road away from both the castle and Karak. The woman wore a long black robe and head scarf, the boy carried a basket. Mrs. Pollifax stood on watch until the police arrived, but the man they looked for had vanished.

They were questioned at the castle by a member of the Provincial Public Security Force, and then sent to the police station in Karak for their statements to be taken down in writing and signed. Telephone calls were made to Amman, but in Arabic, so that Mrs. Pollifax had no idea what was said. The Karak policeman was amiable; they were tourists, after all, and carried American passports. Mrs. Pollifax, who had found the body, could truthfully not describe the face of the man who had fled past her, she could speak only of the color of his *kaffiyeh* and the smear of blood on his pale robe. As for Farrell and Joseph, they had been walking behind her and discussing medieval warfare, scarcely aware of the man rushing past them, and only Mrs. Pollifax's cry for help had interrupted their talk. After they signed their statements, the policeman in charge wrote down the name of their hotel and their room and passport numbers, as well as Joseph's address, and told them the police in Amman would be questioning them further on their return to the hotel.

Joseph's face had interested Mrs. Pollifax during this brief interrogation; it had become very stern, lips tight and eyes expressionless. Most of his statements were given in Arabic, but if he did not mention their three mornings at the castle, she knew there was a limit to his loyalty; they would have to either explain to him about Ibrahim, or dispense with his services and rent a car of their own, now that they knew the country better. Or did Joseph guess too much already to let him go, having witnessed Farrell's search of the dead man?

It was Farrell who made the decision on their drive back to Amman. "Joseph," he said, "you don't have to continue with us as our guide if you'd prefer not, because heaven only knows you couldn't have expected *this.*"

Joseph steered the car to the side of the road, cut the engine, and turned to face them. He said, "You thought for a moment—believed—the dead man your friend. *Yet you did not appear to know what your friend would look like.*"

"True," said Farrell.

"And you searched him," he said accusingly. "And you wondered if the man who killed him was your friend."

"Yes," agreed Farrell.

"But I'm not sure the man who ran away killed him," put in Mrs. Pollifax. "You left the room too soon. There was certainly a terrible fight there, but even you, Joseph, saw no blood on the dead man. There *was* blood, though; you weren't there when I examined the back of his head and found a great deal of blood, both there and on his dagger. It's possible that falling against that stone wall killed him."

When they both looked at her blankly, she said, "Oh for heaven's sake, Farrell, tell him why you're here."

Farrell sighed. "I only hope he won't—but I suppose we owe him *some* explanation. Joseph," he said, "I've come to your country to meet a man by the name of Ibrahim—I know no more of him—and if he's lucky enough to get here, he's bringing me a valuable manuscript from a friend of mine in Iraq who died in prison."

Joseph's eyes widened. "A manuscript? You mean a *book*? Is that all?"

"Yes."

"I don't understand," Joseph said, frowning. "Why would this Ibrahim do this? It's dangerous. What book could be that important? And how would a dead man in Iraq know *you*?"

"Because the writer of the book had been my friend for many years," said Farrell. "He used to lecture in the United States, where we met. He is a very well-known, very courageous writer of books. His name is Dib Assen."

"Dib Assen!" echoed Joseph. "*Dib Assen?* But—"

"But what?" asked Mrs. Pollifax gently.

"But we have read his books in university!" he said excitedly. "Everyone knows of him, he is one of *us.*"

He was silent, and neither of them spoke while he digested this information; his face registered amazement, followed by doubt, suspicion, and, at last, curiosity. "It is for this, not a man in Syria, you wait? You are not—not a *spy*?"

"No," said Farrell gravely.

"Do you think the man who killed the Iraqi agent was this Ibrahim?"

Farrell shrugged. "You heard what Mrs. Pollifax found; it'll be up to the police now to decide. He may only have fought with him, as she suggests. This is possible."

"Yes, that is so," admitted Joseph. "But where did he go, whoever he was? He vanished like smoke! Before the police came I went through every room, and Mrs. Pollifax watched the entrance and did not see him. Where did he go?"

He would have gone into hiding, thought Mrs. Pollifax, *and Farrell will have to leave Jordan without ever fulfilling his promise, and what will happen to the manuscript if it truly was Ibrahim?*

"I don't know," Farrell said grimly, "but

I'm going to return to the castle again to-morrow morning—I must, I have to, it's the only place he can find me. Joseph, can you possibly keep this a secret—for the sake of Dib Assen?"

Frowning, Joseph considered this, and then he said firmly, "You must return to-morrow, yes." He added wistfully, "If I could just touch the pages written by such a man! I would be the first to see it, even to read the first words, because they would be in Arabic, yes?"

"Yes," said Farrell guardedly.

Joseph nodded. "I will stay with you as guide, then, and I swear to you I will not speak of this, even to my brother. . . . I will not abandon you. Besides," he added, with a quick, boyish grin, "how can I, when on Friday Hanan hopes to show Mrs. Pollifax her camel, and it would break her heart to not do this. . . ."

He turned the key in the ignition and started the car, and they proceeded on their way to Amman. They had driven a long way in silence when Joseph said, "*The Mask of the Mullah* was my favorite, oh how I loved that book!"

9

Mrs. Pollifax had returned from dinner when she heard a light tap on her door. Opening it she met with a slender man in a well-cut business suit, black hair flecked with gray. Mrs. Pollifax felt that she was becoming a connoisseur of mustaches now, and his looked particularly elegant in an understated way. "Inspector Jafer," he said, "Department of Criminal Investigation. You are Mrs. Pollifax?"

He held out his identification, and she said, "Yes, do come in."

He walked in and sat down in the upholstered chair by the window; she sat on the edge of her bed and said politely, "I'm very glad to see you—there's something we had planned to take to the police today—but I suppose that first you want more information about the man at Karak castle? Except that I can't think of any detail we missed in our statements."

"No?" he said smoothly. "Actually something else has come to our attention that interests us. In you," he added, with a charming smile.

"In me?"

He nodded, saying pleasantly, "We know, of course, that it was you who found the body, and it was you and your companion, as well as your guide, who were briefly interviewed first by the police at Karak castle. However—"

"Yes?" said Mrs. Pollifax when he paused.

"After you left," he continued, "the members of the tour group were interviewed, and it was noted that you had been seen at Karak castle on the morning before, the three of you." Seeing her eyes flicker, he added almost apologetically, "The tour guide . . . You may not have noticed that the same person brought a different group there on both mornings and saw you there."

He had certainly surprised her, and he knew it; he was, she thought, a very good actor with excellent timing. "Naturally," he continued, "under such circumstances—the investigation of a murdered man from one of our foreign embassies— this seems a curious coincidence."

Curious indeed, she thought, and realized at once that it was up to her to protect Farrell and his purpose in being there, and to protect the unknown man who had fled the scene and might be Ibrahim. She said, "We were there because we were tired of being followed, and Mr. Farrell being an artist—"

"Followed?"

"Yes, and my room has been searched." Carefully she told her story, her eyes on Inspector Jafer's face. "I should have gone to the police earlier, after my room was searched, but I didn't understand why it was done, or why we were followed, until I remembered the man who sat next to me on the plane from New York."

Inspector Jafer sighed but he said courteously, "The man on the plane," and then, lightly, mockingly, "There was a man on a plane?"

She could scarcely blame him for looking skeptical; since it had happened to *her,* she believed it, but hearing herself badly describe what had taken place, she realized it sounded like something out of a low-budget B movie. "I think," she said with dignity, "that it's time I turned over to you what was placed in my carry-on bag while I was in the lavatory brushing my teeth."

"Drugs, perhaps?"

"It's in my money belt for safekeeping, if you'll excuse me for a moment? And it is *not* drugs."

She walked into the bathroom, where she released the money belt from around her waist. Carrying it back into the room, she unzipped it and brought out the key wrapped in paper. Handing it to him she said, "There was this key, and words written on this tissue paper in Arabic. Perhaps you can tell me what they say?"

He carefully placed the key on the arm of the chair and glanced at the diagram, and then pocketed both. "Where did you get these?" he asked.

"I told you, it had to have been dropped into the bottom of my carry-on bag while I was out of my seat on the plane. By the man sitting next to me."

"How do you know it was the man sitting next to you that did this?"

She said patiently, "Because I was on the aisle, and there was no one else next to me. Also, while we talked, he showed me the plaque in which we found the key, and it was the plaque—"

"What plaque?"

"At the moment it's hidden under a pillow in Mr. Farrell's room. A Petra carving mounted on thick plywood, and the key was in the plywood."

"I would like to see that plaque," he said, "but since you tell me you and this man talked together, did he by chance give you his name?"

"Oh yes, and unfortunately I told him mine, too. He introduced himself as Mr. Nayef."

"Nayef," repeated Inspector Jafer, and bringing out a notebook, scribbled down the name. "And how did you happen to find this key in what you describe as a thick slab of plywood?"

Fortunately they were interrupted by a knock on the door; Farrell walked in, startled to find that she was not alone. She said brightly, "Farrell, this gentleman is from the Department of Criminal Investigation. . . . It seems one of the tour guides at the castle today saw us there yesterday, as well as today, which Inspector Jafer has found curious. I have *told* him," she emphasized, meeting Farrell's eyes and holding them, "that we were taking refuge there because we were tired of being followed by that dark red car, and we think the car, and my room being searched, is because of Mr. Nayef." She gestured toward her guest. "I have given him the key from the plaque."

"Thank heaven," said Farrell, with such fervor that the inspector looked startled.

"You are related?" he inquired, looking puzzled.

"Cousins," she announced. "We often travel together. Mr. Farrell is an artist, currently with a gallery in Mexico City, and he is very interested in the ruins here. He's been making drawings of Karak castle and will probably go back tomorrow to finish. He plans to write an illustrated article on your country."

Farrell looked gratified at this; obviously

he could see where this was leading and wanted nothing to do with it. "I'll get the plaque," he said. "It's in my room."

"I'll go with you," said the inspector firmly. "I'm curious as to how you came to find such a key so well hidden."

Mrs. Pollifax smiled at Farrell. "That," she said, feeling she'd already done her part, "is all yours to explain, dear Farrell."

Once alone Mrs. Pollifax locked her door and, with a glance at her watch, laid out her pajamas on the bed and walked into the bathroom. It seemed an appropriate moment to brush her teeth, since so much of her explanations to the inspector had involved a toothbrush, but Mr. Nayef no longer occupied her mind; she was relieved at having so conveniently gotten rid of Mr. Nayef's key, and she had also outflanked the inspector on further questions about their several mornings at Karak castle. She was, in fact, feeling quite virtuous.

She thought now about the dead man found in the dark room of the castle and the man who had rushed past her and vanished. She remained baffled by the mystery of his disappearance. She wondered if he would dare approach the castle again, but of course she also wondered if he had been Ibrahim.

How, she thought crossly, *did he do it?* He had raced past her in such haste that she'd seen little of him, and yet she had been aware of his features distorted in horror. Like Munch's painting *The Scream,* she reflected, and except for that small detail, what had left an impression most clearly was the blood on his robe.

Robe—on his robe . . . Why did this cause a frown? It bothered her, why?

She put down her toothbrush and thought about this, asking herself why the word "robe" was sending out suspicious flashes. She thought crossly, *My subconscious is once again sending messages.* And then, abruptly, she realized that a possibility was being presented to her. There was something overlooked, scarcely credible, and yet . . .

She left her room and knocked on Farrell's door. "Farrell, it's me," she called.

He opened the door, handsome in red silk pajamas, a map in one hand. "What's happened? I gave the inspector the plaque."

"That's not why I'm here," she said. "Farrell, tell me exactly what you saw this morning when you left the castle with that tour guide and walked over to the bus. You looked around, I saw you."

Apparently he didn't think her completely mad. Closing his eyes to remember, he said crisply, "The tour bus, the black car, and Joseph's taxi."

"And?"

He opened his eyes. "You want more? Mountains, gravel, sand, a few stunted trees, the road winding back to town, a woman in black from head to foot, walking with a boy in the opposite direction."

"Exactly," she said, "but where did they come from?"

He looked blank. "The woman and the boy? I don't know. A house?"

"I didn't see any houses up that way," she told him. "If they'd come from the town, we would have passed them on the way. They didn't arrive in a car. Joseph gave me *very* poor directions about getting to the top of the castle, and while I was looking for a second set of stairs anyone could have walked out of the castle, including that woman and the boy."

He said in astonishment, "My God, Duchess, you're not suggesting—?"

"It's just a thought," she said with a smile. "After all, it wasn't so long ago that I was a bag lady. Interesting what a disguise can accomplish, don't you think?"

She left him looking thoughtful, and returning to her room, she changed quickly into her pajamas, climbed into bed, and turned out the light. Having found the day far more eventful than expected, she immediately fell asleep.

10

It was decided the next day that Farrell would spend his morning at the castle with his sketchbooks, and Joseph and Mrs. Pollifax would drive to the Dead Sea, after which they would return for Farrell. "But first," said Mrs. Pollifax, with a pointed glance at Farrell, "Joseph and I will take a walk up the road."

"Walk?" said Joseph. "Not drive?"

"Not drive."

"Let me know if anything turns up, it's important I be here. If nothing, see you at noon," Farrell told her.

As they began their walk up the unpaved road, Joseph said, "Mr. Farrell remains full of hope?"

"He's very stubborn," she told him, "but I fear that he grows a little desperate by now, having come so far to meet this man."

"Yes," Joseph said seriously, "he has come *very* far. And to think that he has been a friend of Dib Assen! And *what* a friend! We have a saying in my country that 'A friend is a second self and a third eye.' I look upon Mr. Farrell with honor. . . . May I ask what we are looking for on this walk, Mrs. Pollifax?"

"For a house—a hut—a hiding place. Anywhere that a man could hide, namely the man who escaped us after leaving the castle yesterday."

"But there was no one leaving the castle!" protested Joseph. "No one seen at all."

"On the contrary," she said, "there was a woman all in black and a small boy that I saw walking up this road, and that Farrell also saw."

Joseph shot her an appreciative glance. "And you think—you think that perhaps the man we are looking for had a black robe and *burqa* waiting?"

"I don't know," she told him, "but they were the only two people on the road, and they weren't in sight when we arrived at the castle."

Joseph grinned. "You think like a detective, Mrs. Pollifax. Hanan has two very, very old torn copies of books about a girl named Nancy Drew. Maybe you too are a Nancy Drew?"

"Somewhat older," she remarked dryly.

They had walked some distance from the castle when Joseph halted, staring off to the right at a small rise in the ground. "Someone was there," he said, pointing.

She saw nothing but followed him across the bare and graveled earth, wondering what had caught his eye. "Look," he said, stopping, and pointed at the ground.

"A pile of ashes . . . a fire?" she asked, frowning.

He thrust his hand into the ashes. "Still a little warm. And look here—*wallah!*—a posthole. There should be others." He walked around, studying the earth and indicating three other indentations in the gravel, all of these surrounding the heap of gray ashes.

"Someone camped here," he said, "and they have gone. Sometime in the night they left. Gypsies or Bedouin, who knows."

She stood and watched as he circled the hillock, finally nodding. "Two donkeys," he said, "heading south."

"I see nothing," protested Mrs. Pollifax.

Joseph smiled at her forgivingly. "Maybe you think like the American Nancy Drew, but you are not Bedouin. Hanan, she would do even better, but surely you can see this very faint print where the gravel turns to sand? This is the print of a donkey. And look—here is his dung—but now the ground grows hard, and there is no way to follow where they went; only Awad Ibn Jazi would have the eyes to follow the tracks."

"Hanan's friend?"

He nodded. "She learns from him, he was—is—a famous tracker."

"But people were here?" she repeated. "Gypsies or Bedouin?"

"Yes. A very small tent, a small camp, but there was a fire, for warmth and cooking. No women, or the tent would have been larger, with a *muharram*."

"But—*could* it have been Ibrahim?"

He said tactfully, "How is that possible? He is not *bedu,* is he?"

"No," she sighed. "Or a gypsy. But if the woman in black was really a woman, where did *she* go?"

He shrugged. "She has left no prints, who can tell?" Seeing her disappointment he said gently, "Gypsies, they come and go, you know. She may have had business with them."

"Yes," she said, with a sigh. There was nothing else to be seen, and they returned to the car and began their drive to the Dead Sea, followed discreetly by a dull red sedan.

When they returned at 12:15 to the castle, Farrell was seated outside in the sun, waiting for them and looking glum.

"No one came?" she said.

"Swarms of police were here for about an hour. Inspector Jafer even came up to watch me sketch—probably to make sure I wasn't lying," he said grimly. "Useless to have come this morning. You saw the Dead Sea?"

She nodded. "It was very white, and so

hot that once out of the car I thought I might faint. We sat in the air-conditioned rest house and watched braver people walk down to the shower rooms and the sea."

"Duchess, we're not doing too well, are we?" Farrell said ruefully.

"We need a change," she told him firmly. "Joseph would like to show us Jerash, some miles north of Amman, but I find I don't want to see any more ruins just now, I want to see people. He's invited us to his house, and Farrell, his mother has a *garden.*"

Joseph nodded. "Ever since Hanan met you, she speaks of you; I know my mother would like to meet you. She doesn't say so, but she fusses a little about Hanan going tomorrow to the desert—with me, of course, but also two strangers. I'm sure she'd like very much to know you."

"Well, I've certainly seen enough of Karak castle," Farrell said bitterly. "I'm rather tired of ruins myself. Incidentally, did the red car show up?"

"Of course," said Mrs. Pollifax. "They're devoted to us. We were followed down and back, except they disappeared once we neared Karak, but I'm sure they're not far away."

But even this didn't interest Farrell.

"The most surprising thing to me about the Dead Sea," she announced, "was that the opposite bank of the sea belongs to Israel. I can't get over how close all these countries are to each other!"

This received no response from Farrell, either.

"You're depressed," she told him. "Let's go, Joseph. Mr. Farrell needs cheering up, and I need a garden. . . ."

Mrs. Pollifax approved at once of the house in which the Jidoors lived. It was two-storied, on a busy street, with a balcony on the second floor from which baskets of flowers hung, and Mrs. Pollifax liked flowers. The house looked squeezed on either side by neighbors, but after they passed through a living room with couches and chairs and a television set, its walls bare except for a picture of King Hussein, they discovered the walled yard behind it was capacious and productive.

A grape arbor lined one wall; there were neat rows of beans and cabbage and eggplant, a clothesline, a plastic greenhouse filled with tomatoes, and even more pots of flowers. The surface around the back door had been paved; chairs were scattered across this small terrace, and it held what looked to be an outdoor oven.

Obviously this was the heart of the house, decided Mrs. Pollifax. The woman picking cucumbers looked up and, seeing Joseph, called out, *"Masch' Allah, Youseff! Taib!"*

He called out to her in Arabic and she walked toward them smiling, her cheerful round face flushed from the sun, saying *"Ahlan wa sahlan."*

"Umm," he said, "they are American, you must speak English because I have brought you Mrs. Pollifax and Mr. Farrell."

But Mrs. Pollifax, courtesy of the nefarious Mr. Nayef, said, *"As salam alaikum!"*

"Very nice," she said approvingly.

"She wants to see your garden," Joseph told her.

His mother beamed with pleasure. "Yes, yes, but first tea—and with *sukar*—

sugar—and would you like mint? Sit, please!"

Chairs were pulled up to a table, and Joseph's mother disappeared into the house to return with tiny cups of tea on a tray and a plate of pastries drenched in honey; at once Farrell began to look more cheerful. As for Mrs. Pollifax, she found it lovely to sit in the sun and relax; it was peaceful, as gardens always were, and she'd not realized how tension had been mounting without her becoming aware of it. Yesterday had tightened nerves that she could feel thawing now, and as if Joseph's mother saw this, she gave her a friendly nod. "It is *taib*—good?"

"Very *taib*," said Mrs. Pollifax. "And we have your permission for Hanan to join us tomorrow and show us her camel?"

"Ah, that Hanan!" exclaimed Mrs. Jidoor, laughing. "She will show you many camels."

"In her cowboy boots," Farrell said, grinning.

Mrs. Jidoor nodded vigorously, "She will be here from school very presently and you will see her."

Joseph smiled. "She has many plans

for you; she first wishes you to meet Awad
Ibn Jazi, who lives in the small village of
Arb'een, near the King's Highway. She
hopes he may drive us in his pickup truck
across the desert to our grandfather. But
also," he added wryly, "she wishes Awad
to show you the half-buried fort that he
knows about from his days in the *badiya*."

"She hasn't seen it?"

"Once, three or four years ago, Awad
showed it to her," said Joseph. "She was
very young, and she would never be allowed to ride out and look for it again, too
many things can happen in the desert; a
camel may go lame, one may get lost,
carry too little water . . . and who
among us has time to go with her? Our
grandfather has many sheep, he is *rich* in
sheep and head of our tribe, with many
responsibilities."

Mrs. Pollifax, startled, said, "Does that
mean—are you saying your grandfather's
a sheikh?"

Joseph nodded proudly. "Yes, but we
call it *shaykh.*"

"Well—there you are, Duchess!" said
Farrell. "Your first *shaykh.*"

Mrs. Pollifax remembered Switzerland

and a playboy sheikh named Yazdan Kashan, who had tried very hard to dispose of her, but she only smiled and said to Mrs. Jidoor, "I'd like to see your garden now." Leaving Farrell—who promptly fell asleep in the sun—the two women moved into the garden to inspect each row and indulge themselves in garden talk.

In midafternoon Hanan arrived home in her school uniform and was astonished at the sight of them. "You are *here*!" she cried excitedly, waking Farrell with a start. "You wish to go *now*?"

Her mother walked toward her, chiding her sternly in Arabic, and Hanan stammered, "*Assif—afwan!* I mean sorry—excuse me. Please!"

Farrell, catching Mrs. Pollifax's eye, said, "We could, you know."

"Could what?"

"Go now." He shrugged helplessly. "What's here for me, after all? It's turning out to be quite hopeless; I've spent four mornings at the castle, and if it was Ibrahim the other day, he'll scarcely dare return. Would *you*? What's more, the inspector mentioned to me this morning—with some crossness, I might add—that representatives from the Iraqi Embassy demand to see the room at the castle where their man was killed. The place will be swarming with officials, off and on."

"Oh dear," said Mrs. Pollifax, wincing. "Your trip here was for nothing?"

He sighed. "What else can I think? But somehow I can't leave yet, not carrying such a heavy sense of failure. Not yet at least. I'm not used to failure, I admit, and since we've three more days before our flight home, maybe I can get rid of the sour taste of this, Duchess. Call it a vacation, maybe. Besides," he added, recovering his humor, "after seeing you on a horse, I'd really enjoy seeing how you manage a camel."

She laughed, but she was not fooled.

"So what do you say?" Turning to Joseph, he said, "Can we go with Hanan now? It'll be light for some hours yet."

"You are restless," Joseph said shrewdly, and nodded. "I feel your discouragement and share it, for I too had so hoped—but yes, we could go now, at least as far as Arb'een before darkness comes, and that is where Awad Ibn Jazi lives."

"What should we pack and take?" asked Mrs. Pollifax, thinking this was just the thing, an excellent antidote to Farrell's gloom and her worry about him. It would be like going on a picnic, or an overnight camping trip, a delightful venture into the unknown and a relief from the events of the last several days.

"Sweaters for the night," said Joseph. "Clothes for riding. Sandals? Sunglasses. Hanan, go and pack your kit and fetch the jug for water. . . . We will then drive to the hotel, so Mr. Farrell and Mrs. Pollifax can add what they need, and—we will *go*! Hurry, Hanan."

Mrs. Pollifax gave Farrell a kind glance. "We will have an adventure," she told him. "It will be relaxing."

Hanan had disappeared. Farrell, playing the good sport, lifted one of the empty teacups and held it up. "To Hanan's desert, then . . ."

11

Inspector Jafer was anything but relaxed. Back from his visit to Karak castle that morning, he sat in his office reflecting on the complications of a foreigner—and an Iraqi at that—found dead in Karak. His men had returned there to photograph again and measure the dimensions of the small room, and they had found added drops of blood that had seeped into the earthen floor. But while an incensed Iraqi embassy called it murder, the inspector was not so sure. Tests on blood samples, taken yesterday from the dead man, had established that they did not match the blood staining the dagger, still fixed in his hand by rigor mortis, as they were of a very different blood type, O. . . . Jafer had begun to suspect that the dead Iraqi had been the aggressor, had attempted to kill the man he'd attacked, and that the blood on the dagger belonged to his mysterious victim who had disappeared. It was proving difficult to convince the embassy that the only wound inflicted on the dead man, whose name was Fareeq Chalki, was the contusion on the back of his head, where it had struck the wall. Someone had fought hard, knocking him down, and it was the inspector's growing conclusion that this was what had killed him. He was quite sure that tests on the samples of blood taken from the floor and wall would confirm that they were *not* Fareeq Chalki's, and the Iraqi would not like this at all.

He sighed. Jordan preserved an extremely delicate balance in the Middle East. After long decades of anti-Israel anger the king had signed a peace treaty with Israel, and this did not sit well with Jordan's Islamic conservatives who made up the opposition. During the Persian Gulf War, Jordan had maintained a supportive relationship with Iraq, although lately this had cooled, especially since Saddam's two sons-in-law and his daughters had defected to Jordan and had been granted asylum by the king. In Jordan, their presence had met with indifference from other Iraqi defectors, who distrusted them, and after six months they had stunned the world by appealing to Saddam, who promised them forgiveness, and by returning to Iraq, where three days later they were murdered. Saddam had not forgiven them after all; would he forgive Jordan for giving them asylum? The situation was worrisome. The Gulf War had earned them new enemies and had cost them a great deal: unemployment was high; they remained in the awkward position of depending upon Iraq for oil imports, but also on the allied countries—and the United States in particular—for economic aid. Their wise and resourceful king had walked such a tightrope for more than forty years, but now this had happened; just when they could ill afford an irate neighbor; in fact, at this moment Iraq, rising like a phoenix from the ashes of war, was moving its troops around in a very provocative manner, which puzzled and worried the United States as well as Jordan.

He sighed. He had made a full report to his superior of what his men had found at Karak castle, the details only a little more comprehensive than the report his chief would have received from the police at Karak. To this he had added his interview in Amman with the woman who had discovered the body, taking care to describe the curio she said had been given her on the flight to Jordan without her knowing it. Usually it was hashish, not a curio, that was planted on traveling tourists, a habit that customs was very apt at discovering, but a curio was something of an oddity. He remained puzzled, though, as to how she and her friend had learned the plaque concealed a key. "Fell on the floor and it broke open," Mr. Farrell had told him, which was scarcely credible, but he'd accepted it for the moment. It had been even more difficult to accept the woman's tale of being followed by a dark red sedan, and he'd put it down to paranoia, until both Farrell and the guide, Joseph Jidoor, had confirmed this.

Without comment he'd fully reported all this in his statement, detailing as well the woman's explanation of how she was sure the plaque had been dropped into her carry-on bag by a man seated next to her named Nayef. Jafer had dropped the key and the tissue paper into an envelope, labeled it, and placed it in his desk. Eventually his superior would read his report, but he had been occupied all morning fielding calls from the Iraqi embassy. However, he'd scheduled a conference for the department at five o'clock.

It was four o'clock when his chief virtually burst into his office, brandishing Jafer's report and looking almost apoplectic.

"Sir?" Jafer said, rising from his desk.

"Nayef," sputtered his superior.

"Nayef?"

He rattled the pages of the report. "This woman says the man next to her on the plane from New York called himself *Nayef*?"

Inspector Jafer nodded.

"We've just heard from Intelligence that Suhair Slaman was on a flight out of New York on Sunday using the name of Nayef."

Jafer's mouth dropped open. "*Suhair

Slaman!" he gasped. "*Bismallah,* the woman spoke the truth?"

"Apparently, yes," his chief said grimly. "I've delivered personally your report to the director general; now let's see what you have here. . . . The man disembarked in Amsterdam, but there are suspicions that his business in the United States concerned Jordan, and since we know of his involvement in at least two of the assassination attempts on our king, this is bad news. If he left the plane at Amsterdam, he need only have caught the next flight to Istanbul, and from Istanbul a direct flight to Damascus, and in Syria he has many friends. *Now where is that souvenir plaque and key?*"

Jafer reached into his top drawer and drew out the broken plaque and the envelope labeled "Exhibit 5032." "Here is the key. They tell me it was wrapped in this thin slip of paper that has a date and mysterious lines that look—well, you tell me."

Studying it, his chief said, "I certainly don't like the date written here. . . . *Ishreen al awal, talateen . . .* October 30 . . . Have you forgotten? The president of Egypt arrives the twenty-ninth, and on the thirtieth he and King Hussein review the air force training exercises in the company of Quidat al-Am, senior officer of the military services." He scowled at the diagram. "This could tell us something of their plans, perhaps? Jafer—"

The inspector sprang from his chair. "Sir?"

"Call the office of the director general of Intelligence, tell them we've found the key and the plaque mentioned in your report, then meet me in the map room. Call Sadrātī in Decoding and bring him with you. And this woman—" He glanced at the report. "—this Mrs. Pollifax, we'll need her, but—no time for that yet, assign two good men to keep her under surveillance as of *now,* and tell them we want to learn who's in that red car. We want that car, Jafer."

"Yes, sir."

As his chief hurried out of the room Jafer rang Intelligence, and then his assistant, asking for Tūhamī and Nāsirī, and gave them his orders. "Pollifax," he told them. "P-o-l-l-i-f-a-x. Room 310, Continental Hotel." He added a description of her and of Mr. Farrell and described what he knew of the dark red sedan following Jidoor's taxi, and then rang Sadrātī in Decoding, after which he hurried to the map room.

"They're stepping up the border patrol," were the first words that met them when they gathered in the map room. "Before sending this over to Intelligence, Sadrātī, see what you can make of these—" He frowned over the slip of paper. "I can only call them scribbles with lines."

Sadrātī found a desk and sat down. Bringing out a magnifying glass, he began studying the tangle of O's that were arranged in an interesting pattern, with three arrows pointing to their center and a horizontal line below. After a long silence Sadrātī said, "I doubt this is a code. I'm thinking these clusters of circles could be trees or shrubs, the three slanting arrows leading into the center of them the means of entry, and this long line below a road. What are you suspecting here?"

"Something planned for October 30, possibly an assassination attempt," the inspector told him.

Sadrātī whistled softly through closed

teeth. "Then I suggest an aerial map. If we could possibly find a similar design of trees, or even small buildings at some important point, with this bottom horizontal line denoting a highway or road—"

"It's worth a try," said the inspector. "But hurry."

They spread out the aerial maps and the three men pored over them. Sadrātī made a tracing of the series of O's, and they moved it about, looking for a match.

"Whoever was to receive this—whoever hoped to steal it from this Mrs. Pollifax," pointed out Inspector Jafer, "would understand precisely what these marks mean. That makes it vital that we interrogate the men who are following her in the red sedan."

"I agree, yes," his chief said grimly, "but they could be only subordinates or mere hirelings."

"At least there's time in our favor," he was reminded. "This is—what, the thirteenth? And the date here for whatever is planned is October 30."

"Nothing is certain when it's Suhair Slaman behind it."

"Suhair Slaman!" exclaimed Sadrātī. "Merciful Allah, you didn't tell me *that*. You say there is a woman involved in this?"

Jafer nodded. "An American tourist who happened to be the recipient of this key without knowing it—at least until her room was searched and she realized that she was being followed."

Sadrātī's gaze was accusing. "You say there is much time between now and October 30, but there is bound to be a day—long before that—when they close in on this woman and demand the key."

"It is our good fortune," pointed out the chief, "that they still believe that she has it."

Sadrātī looked at him in horror. "Mercifully I deal only in codes and deciphering, but do you think any terrorist would believe her when she tells them she doesn't have what they want? You are surely exposing her to much danger!"

"We're not fools," the inspector told him curtly. "If we bring her in too soon, we lose all hope of capturing and interrogating the two men who follow her in the red sedan. We'll be giving her every protection. . . . I've just sent two of my best men to the hotel with orders to keep her under constant surveillance. . . . Now let's get back to the business at hand."

They returned to the aerial map, concentrating on vulnerable sites: on the King Hussein Air Base; the King Abdullah Air Base, and the Palace. But a cluster of trees or buildings placed where any activity would take place on October 30 proved impossible to find on such a huge aerial map.

"It's useless," said Jafer, and his chief nodded. "We have the date, however, and we have this key."

"Not enough," said the chief, "but something. And we have this Mrs. Pollifax. We do, don't we, Jafer?"

"I'll check," he said, and going to the phone, spoke to his assistant. "I can report that my men are stationed at the hotel now, sir. Mrs. Pollifax and her cousin have been out all day, and both of their room keys have been left at the front desk. The dining room opens at seven-thirty and it has been their custom to dine at the hotel."

The chief nodded. "Good. And now you'd better take the contents of the plaque to Intelligence."

When Inspector Jafer had gone, Sadrātī said thoughtfully, "Can you really believe, sir, that Suhair Slaman will personally come back to Jordan, whatever is planned? He escaped last time just minutes before arrest, and he's well known to the Desert Patrol, the army, and the police."

The chief gave a bitter laugh. "Hard to believe, yes, but from what Intelligence has learned, he entered the United States last week, spent three days there, and left without being recognized."

This drew a whistle from Sadrātī. "*Hada 'atel!* This is bad."

"Very bad. And this key? I wish Intelligence success. It will be like—what is that American expression?—looking for a needle in a stack of hay."

"What do you do now?" asked Sadrātī curiously.

"We are still in charge of a murder investigation, and we will continue our in-

vestigation, and when this Mrs. Pollifax
returns to the hotel we will learn more,
much more. The rest—'' He shrugged.
''The rest is up to Intelligence now.''

12

Driving down the Desert Highway—followed as usual by the distant red sedan—Mrs. Pollifax and Farrell experienced their first sampling of desert country. They had left Karak behind them when Joseph suddenly slowed the car, and drawing off to the side of the road he said simply, "See the sky—sandstorm! I suggest *there*," and he pointed to the only building nearby, a shabby roadside restaurant. As they climbed out of the car he said, "Hurry!"

Others had already taken refuge inside, where there was a scattering of plastic tables and chairs, and a counter where soda, chips, candy, and cigarettes were sold. There was no sign of the red sedan. Farrell bought Hanan a soda and they stood at the window to watch the sky grow progressively more yellow. The wind had risen, searching out dust and debris at the roadside and scattering it playfully, tossing small objects over and over until they disappeared from sight.

A delivery truck pulled into the parking area, followed by a black sedan, and peering closely at the latter, Farrell said, "That Volvo . . . Duchess, the man in the backseat, do you see him? He looks like the man who talked Arabic literature to me in the hotel dining room."

"The Man in the Black Silk Suit?" Following his glance, Mrs. Pollifax saw only a shadowed face before the storm bore down on them, rendering Joseph's car and the Volvo completely invisible under an onslaught of yellow dust. She shook her head. "Sorry, I didn't recognize him."

"Is he coming in here? Damn it, no," growled Farrell, "he and the driver are sitting out the storm in the car. But Duchess, I *swear*—"

"But not in front of Hanan," she teased him with a smile.

"You," he announced, "are not taking me seriously. All right, I'll be quiet."

The wind blew steadily for half an hour, and then, as abruptly as it had overtaken them, it slackened; Joseph's car became visible, the black Volvo drove away, the sky slowly cleared and was blue again, and they resumed their drive to Arb'een. But now, perversely, Farrell's concern about the man in the Volvo returned to plague Mrs. Pollifax. She was remembering what Farrell had so far overlooked: the unclaimed black car parked at Karak castle on the morning of the murder that had to have belonged to either the dead Iraqi, or to the man who had run away. . . . Yet, if the car had belonged to the man who fled, he need only have jumped into it and quickly escaped them, but the car was still there when they had left the castle with the police. The next morning it had been removed, and she wondered by whom: the police, or by someone from the Iraqi embassy?

Of course there had to be dozens of black Volvos in Amman alone, she reminded herself, and the Man in the Black Silk Suit had every right to be traveling anywhere he pleased, but he was also the man at the hotel who had maneuvered his conversation on Arabic literature so that it included Dib Assen.

Coincidence or not?

She shook her head. . . . The connection was too vague to speak of to Farrell, and she returned her attention to the present moment. Hanan, in the front seat beside her brother, was chattering away about horses: it seemed that her admired friend Qasim had a new, purebred bay with black points, a white foot, and a blaze on its face. He had shown it to her when she'd last visited her grandfather several weeks ago. At that time, she said, turning to confide this to Mrs. Pollifax and Farrell, there had been many tents and many guests, all coming south for the winter.

Joseph laughed. "Maybe you do not know how welcoming we *bedu* are, it is a law of the desert."

"I've heard of that," Farrell told her. "Friend or enemy is given food and a bed—at least for three days, isn't it?"

Joseph shrugged. "For any friend of Youseff and Hanan there is no such law. My grandfather will kill a sheep for you and give a *mansef*—a feast."

Oh dear, thought Mrs. Pollifax, *I do hope the eyes of the sheep are no longer a great delicacy.*

"We are very near to Arb'een now," Joseph said. "Arb'een means forty. They say it was named this years and years ago, but nobody any longer knows why. Forty miles to *somewhere,* probably to a well, or to a town, but the nearest town is Sad as Sultanī, and is *not* forty miles away."

Hanan said firmly, "Awad says a *well.*" Obviously her loyalties to a friend were staunch and invincible.

Joseph laughed. "All right, then, a well."

It was nearly dusk when they drew up to the house of Awad Ibn Jazi. If Arb'een was a village, it was a tiny one, no more than a cluster of houses, like a way station. As they left the car and walked into the front yard, Mrs. Pollifax heard the cooing of doves and saw a dovecote set high into the wall, and she smiled. The front of the square cement house was shaded by fruit trees, and the walk to the front door was paved with flat stones painted in pastel colors of blue, turquoise, and pink.

The sound of their voices brought a man to the door, a small man, a little bent, his face like polished brown leather with a network of cracks and seams, his eyes bright and shrewd and suddenly full of warmth when they saw Hanan. He wore a gray robe with a checkered *kaffiyeh* bound with a black cord, or *aigal,* and his feet were in sandals. Both Hanan and Joseph halted to greet him formally with a ritual of questions and replies in Arabic: *keef halak,* how are you . . . *al-hamdu lillah,* fine, thanks be to God, and then Joseph said, "We have brought you two Americans, Awad Ibn Jazi. It is Hanan's desire they meet our grandfather tomorrow."

The man glanced at Mrs. Pollifax and Farrell, measuring and weighing them knowledgeably before he said, "*Ahlan wa sahlan—faddal!*"

"They're American," Joseph reminded him, grinning.

"Then I am saying to you: I welcome you, please come in." He smiled broadly, showing a gap between his front teeth and continuing in English, "And no doubt little Hanan wishes you to see her white camel."

Mrs. Pollifax laughed. "Oh yes, indeed!"

"You can take us there tomorrow?" Joseph asked Awad, with hope in his voice.

Awad sniffed at the question. "Would I like anything better? Already I tire of walls!"

With this established they became aware of small children peering at them from behind Awad. Advancing into the house they also met with a handsome and stately young woman in a black robe, "Awad's granddaughter Rehab," whispered Joseph, and the names of the children were flung at them: the girls were Ghada, Saadija, and Nawal, and the little boy, Tahar, children of Rehab and her absent husband, Omar. Mrs. Pollifax was startled to realize they all lived in this tiny three-room house. They stood awkwardly in the living room, feeling surrounded. It was a small room with a television set, a pile of neatly stacked mattresses in one corner, and a jumble of benches and pillows. Rehab brought two chairs from the rear yard and began issuing what sounded like orders in Arabic.

Joseph, translating, said, "She is sending Ghada next door to her sister's house to borrow more rice for our dinner, and since it is too cold to sleep on the roof she orders Saadija to carry mattresses to the room upstairs for Hanan and you, Mrs. Pollifax. And she reminds Awad there is a movie from Egypt on the television tonight to entertain you."

Mrs. Pollifax said quickly, "Please thank her and apologize to her for this inconvenience."

"No problem," Joseph said. "We will have a good dinner, there will be *kusa mahshi*, and Rehab promises it in one hour and one half."

Farrell, with a glance at his watch, nodded. "At seven-thirty, then . . . Seven-thirty is a very elegant hour to dine in the United States, although early in Mexico. Please thank her!"

13

At that same hour Inspector Jafer, in Amman, was waiting to hear from his two men stationed at the hotel, ready to begin their surveillance assignment on Mrs. Pollifax and her cousin. A number of events were now being woven into a substantial and dangerous pattern as more news came in. Intelligence, for instance, had known for several days of the robbery and death of Brahim Zayyad in Washington, D.C., on October 7, but not immediately as to whether the murder was random or premeditated. His wallet and certain other items had been stolen, but it had taken time to learn just what could be missing other than money.

The report from the Americans that Suhair Slaman had been in the United

States on the seventh and left on the eighth had at once added an ominous dimension. This news had reached Jafer from Hugh Rawlings in the CIA office in Amman. From Jordanian Intelligence he had also learned that Brahim Zayyad was not only a high-level officer in Palace Security, but that he carried certain keys on his person at all times—in Jordan, at least—and since the keys were missing, it was being feared that he must have carelessly, or absentmindedly—or naively—worn them on his person when he flew to the United States for ten days as a consultant on the embassy's security.

It was apparent now that *someone* had learned that the keys had left the country with Zayyad and had informed Suhair Slaman's group. A rigorous investigation was already in progress as to who might have been privy to this information, and what person in the palace could be a secret member of Slaman's terrorist group. Heads would soon roll on *that* score, he hoped.

By six o'clock the key that Mrs. Pollifax had turned over to Inspector Jafer had been identified, but Palace Security would say no more than that. It was nearly eight o'clock when he received the phone call from Tūhamī. They had been taking turns watching the registration desk and the cubicles containing the keys for rooms 308 and 310, he said, and when the dining room opened at half past seven, Tūhamī had walked over to the registration desk to again accost the room clerk he'd spoken with earlier.

"Just going off duty," the man had told him. "Still here?"

"Of course we're still here, we're waiting for 308 and 310 to return, you said they dine here."

The clerk had nodded and shrugged. "Yes, but as you can see—the guests are not here."

The cashier, standing several feet away from him under the sign CASHIER, had said, "What's wrong?"

"They wait for rooms 308 and 310, Pollifax and Farrell, to return. A police matter."

The cashier, startled, had said, "But they left long ago. It was to me they handed their keys, and the woman—Pollifax, you say?—said they were keeping their rooms, but would be away overnight."

A lengthy argument had ensued, as to why the cashier had accepted their keys, and had the room clerk really been too busy to serve them, and Tūhamī was describing this to Jafer when Jafer said, "Hold on a minute, another call, it could be important."

It was not important, it was still another call from Hugh Rawlings at the Jordanian CIA office, hoping for more information. *Persistent chap,* Jafer thought wearily, and placed him on hold, too, while he returned to his conversation with Tūhamī.

"Did you learn anything else?" he inquired curtly.

"We questioned the porters after that," said Tūhamī. "Only one of them had been on duty in midafternoon. He had noticed them because they tip well; he said they both climbed into a waiting taxi and left."

"And after that? Anything more?"

Tūhamī sighed. "After that we tossed a coin, a five fil, as to which of us would tell you the bad news."

"You have called me with the bad news," Jafer told him grimly. "*Now trace the guide.* Name of Youseff Jidoor, his address is on the report from the Karak police. Find out the number of his license plate, visit his home; they may know where he was taking them overnight: to Wadi Rum, or Aqaba, perhaps. *'Ajjel—* hurry!''

Furious, he hung up and turned to the other phone line, and forcing himself to speak in a calm voice, he said, "Yes, Rawlings, you are calling for more information? . . .''

If it was eight o'clock in Jordan, it was two o'clock in the afternoon in Langley, Virginia, and Carstairs was becoming apoplectic over still another coup in West Africa and the hint of problems in Macedonia. It sometimes seemed to him the entire world was erupting in a convulsion of nationalism and tribalism, and he was especially outraged when one of his agents was listed as missing in the subsequent chaos and bloodbaths. On this particular day he was relieved to hear that Tuku Adair had escaped Burkina Faso and had reached a hospital in Botswana.

He was also growing increasingly impatient to hear from Hugh Rawlings in the CIA office in Amman. Events were out of the hands of the FBI, now that the action had moved beyond the borders of the United States, and Carstairs had been given the job of keeping in touch with just what information could be learned about Suhair Slaman. The United States had a very real stake in Jordan; it was, so to speak, a door to the Middle East, suitably placed for keeping an eye on Syria, Lebanon, Iraq, and Iran. It had sold Jordan massive amounts of protective armaments and had no interest at all in seeing radicals take over the country and turn it into another Iraq or Iran. The king had already survived fourteen or fifteen attempts to assassinate him, and Suhair Slaman had been the instigator of at least two of them. The question now was what Suhair's plans might be. His group of militants had already terrorized, bombed, and killed enough people in the Middle East. Carstairs found no reason to doubt that the man now had his eye on Jordan again.

It had become urgent to keep abreast of affairs in Amman, and Rawlings had promised to communicate with him once he could extract information from the police or from their intelligence people over there, but there had been no word from him since Carstairs's initial call. The silence was beginning to grate on him; the difference in time was adding to his frustration.

When Bishop shouted from his office, "Rawlings on line three, sir—Amman calling!" Carstairs spoke a fervent "Thank God!" and plucked the phone from its receiver. "Suspense has mounted, Rawlings," he said. "What's up?"

"They're pretty nervous and uptight over here," Rawlings said, "but I've finally gotten through to a few people. Until now there was nothing to report, but it seems they have a clear fix now on the fact that Slaman's hellish group is definitely planning mischief here, and whatever it may be it's set for October 30."

"That's a beginning," said Carstairs. "But what's planned?"

"More than the date, they don't know yet. In fact, the little they've learned was discovered in a damn unusual way. On that plane to Amsterdam last weekend,

Slaman planted a curio—a wooden plaque—on the woman sitting next to him, an American tourist. A rather odd curio that she later found in her carry-on bag. Somehow this plaque broke—no explanation how *that* happened, it's damn sturdy, I've seen it—and inside this little souvenir was a mysterious key, and a slip of paper with the date October 30 and a diagram or map that's being analyzed now."

"The gods are smiling. . . . Go on, I'm listening."

"Yes . . . Well, unfortunately this woman didn't report any of this at once, not until she found the body of a dead Iraqi intelligence agent at Karak castle."

Carstairs, startled, said, "I beg your pardon!"

"Well yes, old chap, a bit hard on her, of course, but that's what brought the police into the picture. While being interviewed by them she mentioned that she was being followed everywhere by a red sedan, and she wondered if what she'd found in her carry-on bag was why her room had been searched and why she was being followed. *That's* when she turned this plaque over to the police."

"Good heavens! But you have the contents now of the curio?"

Rawlings sighed. "Yes, but they seem to have lost the woman; at least she's gone somewhere overnight with her cousin, still followed by the same car, apparently, and they have to find her to find the men following her."

"This is making me a little dizzy," complained Carstairs. "Sounds damn complicated."

"Not really, sir, this woman tourist hasn't checked out of her hotel room in Amman, so she's bound to return. I've just learned they're contacting Jidoor Tours to see if they can find out where she's gone. This Mrs. Pollifax—"

Stunned, Carstairs said, "Mrs. *who*?"

Behind him Bishop burst out laughing, and Carstairs gave him a stern and reproachful glance. To Rawlings he said calmly, "An innocent tourist, yes, but what's this about an Iraqi agent at Karak castle?"

"She and her cousin—"

"Excuse me, but have you the name of this cousin?"

"Somewhere, yes," replied Rawlings. "Ah, here it is—a Mr. Farrell, apparently an artist. Seems they'd been seen at the castle for two mornings in a row, which made the police suspicious and led to a further interview, which is when Mrs. Pollifax turned over—rather late—the contents of the broken plaque."

"I see," said Carstairs, seeing a great deal more than Rawlings. "Any clues as to who killed the Iraqi agent?"

"There was a man seen running away. He brushed past this Mrs. Pollifax, but too quickly for her to give a viable description of him. He's simply vanished."

Carstairs said thoughtfully, "Certainly interesting. Keep in touch, will you? I'll have to ring off now, Rawlings, but I appreciate the update."

He hung up, frowning, and Bishop said in amusement, "Well? Excuse my laughing, but after all—Mrs. Pollifax!"

"Not *quite* a laughing matter," Carstairs said curtly. "Let me think."

Bishop waited, still smiling but silent.

At last Carstairs said, "Obviously Karak

castle is where Farrell was to meet Dib Assen's friend Ibrahim.''

Bishop nodded. "You think it was Ibrahim who killed the Iraqi agent?''

Carstairs shrugged. "The worrisome part of all this is that if it really was Ibrahim who fled the scene, there was a hell of a lot known about his bringing the manuscript out of Iraq into Jordan. It has to mean that he was betrayed; in Baghdad someone *talked.* In which case Ibrahim could have been under surveillance ever since he arrived, or a photograph circulated at the embassy in Amman for them to be waiting for him or looking for him once he crossed the border into Jordan.''

"And they found him?'' murmured Bishop.

"Possibly . . . if it *was* Ibrahim. But you heard Rawlings; the man has vanished. There's the matter of Mrs. Pollifax having been followed, too, and her room searched, presumably on orders from Suhair Slaman. This complicates matters for Farrell, too.'' He shook his head. "I don't like it.''

"No,'' said Bishop, and then, "Why are you staring at me like that?''

Carstairs frowned. "I'm thinking of Antun Mahmoud in Manhattan, with his underground connections in Iraq. It was he who was contacted by *someone* in Baghdad about Farrell, the manuscript, perhaps even about Karak castle."

Startled, Bishop said, "You don't think—surely not Mahmoud?"

Carstairs shook his head. "No, not Mahmoud. In this area I'd trust him completely, but who knows what happened at the other end, in Baghdad? Mahmoud's contact in Iraq, for instance . . . was his or her message intercepted, or the person arrested and interrogated?" He was silent, considering this. Reaching a decision, he said, "Call Ferad in the Middle East Department, and see if he knows where Mahmoud is this week and how to reach him; the man seems to move constantly. Tell Ferad it's important, and Mahmoud—if he prefers—can phone via the Baltimore 'cover' number."

"Is his phone tapped?" asked Bishop.

Carstairs regarded him with amusement; Bishop had never lived life on the run, it was possible that the sole resistance movement he'd ever experienced was avoiding marriage with any of the blondes he collected. He said politely, "He'll use a pay phone, Bishop."

"Oh—sorry." Bishop looked contrite.

Carstairs nodded. "You're forgiven. See what you can do."

"But what about Emily?"

Carstairs considered this. "I would say that with the entire police force looking for Mrs. Pollifax and Farrell, they are bound to be located before Suhair Slaman finds them. Jordan is, after all, a small country. Now go and tackle Ferad!"

It was late afternoon when a call came in, forwarded through Betsy in Baltimore. "Antun," a muffled voice said, and there was the sound of traffic in the background.

By this time Carstairs had reduced his query to as concise an explanation as he found possible. "There's been a problem," he said. "Concerning Farrell."

"Yes."

"*Karak castle,*" he said deliberately, "has been a surprisingly busy place. We've learned that a foreign agent was found dead in one of its rooms yesterday. A man was seen fleeing the room by F and his companion, if you're following me?"

"I am."

"The man who fled has disappeared and is still missing. If it's who I think—and he's gone into hiding—then F's mission has been aborted. But what is suspicious to me is the nationality of the dead man and how he came to be there at all. I'm wondering if your pipeline has become tainted?"

"That," said Mahmoud evenly, "is always, *always* a possibility."

"I won't ask how the information reached you—"

"Two were involved. Secondhand," said Mahmoud cryptically. "I will look into this at once, or as soon as possible. It could be bad news."

"Yes," agreed Carstairs.

"Thank you," Mahmoud said curtly, and hung up.

Bishop, curious, said, "How *do* you suppose he gets news from Iraq?"

"Since Antun doesn't work for us, I don't know and I don't think I'd want to know. The Middle East is Ferad's department, for the moment," said Carstairs. "I can only speculate."

"Like how and what?"

Carstairs sighed. "There have been so many arrests and killings, I'd have to guess that Antun Mahmoud's contact is either a very-high-up official, absolutely beyond suspicion to have survived the continuing arrests—if there are any left like that, which I doubt—or someone virtually invisible that no one notices—for instance, a modest shopkeeper in the souk, or some quiet and obedient bureaucrat who keeps his thoughts to himself."

He considered this, frowning. "Since Jordan changed its policy toward Iraq it's been collecting even more Iraqi defectors, and so many that the king—and this is risky for *him*—has encouraged Iraqi opposition leaders in Amman to open an office. But I doubt Mahmoud would use any of them as a conduit, they're too recent." He shook his head. "No, it would be my guess that Antun's contacts were set up long before he left the country for the United States: a few people he knew personally, and at least one of them lucky enough to survive. It would have to be a man who has decided that his life has more value if he risks it than if he lives in exile. There are men like that . . . and they are the best of men."

"And what will happen now?" asked Bishop.

Carstairs said curtly, "What will happen now is that Mahmoud will move again to a new location. I can guarantee that because this can put him in danger, too. Wherever he is now, he'll be somewhere else in a few hours."

"That fast?" said Bishop, startled.

Carstairs's thoughts went back to a time long ago when he had lived under the code name of Black Jack, and he, too, had moved fast. "Possibly," he said, "in *one* hour."

14

In Arb'een, at the house of Awad Ibn Jazi, Mrs. Pollifax excused herself before the end of the Egyptian film shown on television. There were no subtitles in English. . . . It appeared to be a story full of turgid and overheated declarations of passion, with two seductively clad young women determined to capture a handsome rich man who resembled Rudolf Valentino. There was also a wide-eyed, brave, and innocent young heroine, whom the volatile hero ignored, but Mrs. Pollifax was quite sure that by the end of the film he would realize her worth, and like Cinderella she would be the one to walk off into the sunset with him. Mrs. Pollifax therefore went up to the little room above, and without undressing lay down on the mattress assigned to her and fell asleep.

A mattress on the floor was still a bed, and Mrs. Pollifax had experienced worse, but although she slept well she was aware of activity in the house during the night. Once, opening her eyes, she saw that Hanan's mattress was empty, and later she heard voices downstairs, one of them Farrell's, but she was too tired to be curious. When she woke in the first gray light of dawn, Hanan was asleep on her mattress and the house was quiet; she wondered if she'd dreamed Hanan's departure and the voices.

Tiptoeing downstairs she found Awad's granddaughter Rehab in the kitchen, boiling water on the kerosene stove and spooning yogurt into dishes. She glanced up and smiled. In the living room mattresses were being stacked in the corner by Saadija, and she saw Farrell, outside, emerging from the outhouse.

He did not look cheerful. "Busy night," he said grimly.

"What do you mean?"

"People," he told her. "Awad heard someone prowling around outside, and

Hanan heard *him,* and that woke *me.*
Awad tried showing me their tracks with a
flashlight, but I failed to see any—he's
amazing. One man was the lookout, Awad
says—he stayed in one place—the other
man walked around the house, stopping
at doors and windows until Awad was
heard, and then they left in a hurry. Probably," he added sourly, "in that blasted old
red sedan."

"You really think—? You know, I did
hear voices in the night."

He nodded. "I've had to explain a few
things about you to Awad. He suggests
we leave in an hour for the desert. You
see, they'd already taken the battery out
of Joseph's taxi."

"They *what*?"

"There's no battery. We have to thank
our lucky stars that Awad overheard them
before they disabled his pickup truck,
too."

"But then we would have had to stay
here," she said in a shaken voice. "Like
sitting ducks?"

"Like sitting ducks, yes. We couldn't
have gone far, certainly."

"And they would have come back

and—Oh, if only they *knew,*" she cried. "Knew that we'd found the key and the police have it. Do you realize they have no idea that we ever took apart the plaque?"

"Innocent Tourist again." Farrell sighed.

"And how can we tell them?" she demanded. "They stay so far behind us, they disappear and reappear, there's been no *way* to tell them."

He nodded. "Rather amateur of them, too, always in the same car."

"Scarcely amateur," she said hotly, "if they were hoping to invade Awad's house and harm us."

"But not until they'd clipped our wings and made sure we were trapped. Sorry," he said after a glance at her face. "Don't worry, we'll be leaving soon. Awad's nephew is going to stay in the house with the women while he's gone, and Awad's cousin next door is going to find another battery for Joseph's car."

"We should pay for that," she said firmly.

"Yes. Now have a cup of tea and bring down your carry-on bag. We should be safe in the desert; Hanan says there are always men at her grandfather's tent, and don't forget Awad's a retired policeman and must have a gun or two left over from his Desert Patrol days."

She said uneasily, "Is it as easy to get guns in Jordan as it is in the United States?"

Farrell, glad to change the subject, said, "No, it isn't, which is no doubt why they have such a low crime rate here. According to Joseph, application is made for a gun, followed by a thorough checking and a bit of a wait before the gun can be purchased, at which time the buyer is issued three bullets, no more, he's fingerprinted, and his name entered in a computer." He glanced at his watch. "I'll go and collect my gear now."

Mrs. Pollifax, who had already brought down her bag, wandered over to say good morning to Awad. Slamming down the hood of his truck, he nodded at her. "Okay, no damage."

"Tell me," she said curiously, "how did you know so much, just by looking at the earth?"

He beamed at her appreciatively. "I show you. There is dew even in the desert, you know, and last night a heavy dew.

Come see, the sun has not yet killed the dew.''

She followed him to the beginning of the rough driveway beside the house and knelt beside him as he pointed at the gravel. ''What do you see?''

''Nothing,'' she said frankly, and smiled at him.

''Look again. The gravel still glistens with dew, *na'am*?''

She nodded.

''But you see here—'' He pointed. ''The gravel has been disturbed, there is no dew.''

''You're right, the pebbles are *dry,*'' she said eagerly. ''You mean—''

''*Na'am*—yes. The toe or heel of a boot kicked up the gravel, turning it over. And here—because of the dew—you see two slight depressions where a man stood long enough to send the gravel deeper into the earth?''

''It's difficult to see,'' she conceded, ''but yes, I *think* I see it now.''

He stood and walked farther up the drive to where tufts of wiry grass had pushed their way through the stones. ''And here?''

Triumphantly Mrs. Pollifax said, "A few stalks of the grass have been flattened."

He beamed at her happily. "Yes, a heavy shoe did this. When the sun warms it—all gone." He led her to the back door. "And here?" He gave her a mischievous glance.

"An entire footprint!" she exclaimed.

"*Na'am*—yes, because the desert is not all flint, and here it is sand. I will know this shoe print if I see it again; this is not a sandal but a city shoe. A man of medium height and weight, not so tall as Mr. Farrell but heavier."

"Extraordinary," said Mrs. Pollifax.

She turned as Hanan appeared, carrying a small sack. Released from school clothes, she was wearing a shabby pair of black Turkish pants, a gray tunic that reached to her knees, and, of course, her cowboy boots. Her head of dark thick curls was hidden under a brilliant neon pink kerchief. She said gravely, "Youseff says there was a car following us yesterday. Awad's cousin next door could lend you a robe and a veil if I asked her. As a disguise, you know. She's very religious."

"Is that what Nancy Drew would do?" asked Mrs. Pollifax.

Hanan considered this. "I think so, don't you? The *thobe* and the veil would be very hot for you in the desert, but it would be clever."

"Even cleverer of you to think of it," Mrs. Pollifax told her. "I can see that you will be very helpful in emergencies."

Hanan, glancing at the truck, said regretfully, "Yes, but there's no time. See? Youseff's waving at us, we have to leave now."

"We'll talk later," Mrs. Pollifax assured her, and foreseeing heat and sun, she brought her dark glasses out of her purse and placed an efficient wide-brimmed hat on her head.

It was seven in the morning when they set out on their journey into the desert, and once they left Arb'een behind them it was a rough drive, sometimes over old camel trails, more often leaving those to drive off in a more northerly direction. Because of the incessant bouncing of the truck they took turns between riding in the front, where two could sit, and in the open rear, where there were a few thin pillows to ease the impact of the jolts, but where Mrs. Pollifax found that mostly she slid from side to side at every turn of the wheel. The earth was so persistently brown and uneven that the occasional bushes of green—salt grass, said Hanan—were a refreshing sight. In the distance Mrs. Pollifax could see long smudges of gray that promised a range of mountains, but these were obviously far away; the desert itself remained flat, although not so flat that they were not considerably shaken by small hillocks, and stones that glittered in the sun, and once a dried-up stream bed—a wadi, said Hanan—that had to be crossed and was so steep that Mrs. Pollifax feared the truck would turn over before it crawled up the opposite bank.

It was nearing nine o'clock when Hanan pointed and Mrs. Pollifax saw far ahead a cluster of long black shapes.

"*Buyut sha'ar,*" Hanan said joyfully. "Tents!"

"But what are those hundreds of dots?"

"Dots?" Hanan said, puzzled, and then, "Oh! Sheep and goats, there is good *nassi* to feed on here. The big tent is my grandfather's," she added proudly.

As Awad's pickup truck sputtered and whined its way into the encampment, children came running, dogs barked, women peered curiously from the tents, their faces brightening when they saw Awad and Hanan. The truck came to a stop before the largest of the four tents. It looked low-slung, sagging between its tent poles as if lacking headroom, but the man emerging from it stood tall: a strong face dominated by piercing eyes under thick white brows; a long face with a long nose, a wide and generous mouth and a strong jaw, with a tuft of white beard adorning it. His head wreathed in a *kaffiyeh* that framed his face and extended down to his waist.

"My grandfather," Hanan announced with pleasure.

15

The face of Sheikh Abdul Ibn Jidoor's tent in the desert was open to the breezes that arrived from the east, revealing the tent poles supporting it made of slender saplings. The tent of heavy woven goat hair might be black, but its floor was strewn with brilliant Bedouin and Persian carpets. The women's quarters, or *muharram,* was curtained off and hidden behind an equally bright carpet that hung at one end of the tent, and Hanan disappeared into it, leaving Mrs. Pollifax to realize that because she was a guest of Joseph, and a foreigner, she was to be allowed among the men. She and Farrell were ushered inside. Other than the carpets, the only furnishings were a fire pit in the middle of the space, on which rested an elegant silver urn; a number of plump pillows; and a low table bearing two more urns and a battery-powered radio. Mrs. Pollifax joined the men, seating herself cross-legged, as they did, while one of the younger men brought out a tray of small cups and poured steaming Turkish coffee into them.

After three cups of the thick strong brew, heavily flavored with cardamom, Mrs. Pollifax felt that she could cope with anything, but wished for a toothbrush to remove some of the coffee grounds from her teeth. Denied this she settled down to watching and listening, not without pity for Farrell who sat next to her, but edgily, being unaccustomed to the half-lotus position. She herself was somewhat out of practice, but realized she was earning some respect for accomplishing this from the glances of approval and curiosity she was given. Hanan had told her that her grandfather spoke English, but apparently this was a conference, and not all of the sheikh's men were so endowed.

Following the rounds of coffee they were not to be immediately released, however; two young women carried in dishes of hummus, of mashed eggplant swimming in oil, slices of tomato, and freshly baked *khobz.* Mrs. Pollifax began to wonder just when they were to be shown the half-buried fort that so few people knew about, and that Hanan wanted them to see. After lunch ended, with elaborate thanks to the sheikh, they were joined outside by Hanan, and Mrs. Pollifax questioned her.

It was Joseph who answered. Looking troubled, he said, "I would not wish to go to the fort without my grandfather's consent. I have spoken to him about this trip; he only smiled and nodded and said that he has given orders that a sheep be killed for a feast in your honor tonight."

Farrell said, "But this is Friday, Joseph, and we fly back to the United States late Monday!"

"My grandfather lives by desert time," Joseph said ruefully. "He does not understand such matters. Still, this is not like him." He frowned. "Something worries him, I feel this. About our going."

Mrs. Pollifax, who was quite happy to remain here, said cheerfully, "We don't *have* to see a half-buried fort. There feels something very wrong about rushing about here, just as we do at home. Oh look," she said. "Camels—a string of them! And a man on a horse!"

"It's Qasim," cried Hanan, beaming. "He is bringing me my camel!"

Mrs. Pollifax found herself very interested in this Qasim, and in the relationship between him and eleven-year-old Hanan, so wise beyond her age. She was also a little afraid of meeting him, because if he was to be Hanan's future, she wondered if he would undermine or even destroy the surprise of her, forcing her to conform. He rode toward them on the striking black-and-white bay that Hanan had described, and dismounting, he grinned at Hanan. "Little cousin," he said, "I heard you have guests."

"I have guests, Qasim, yes," she told him primly.

"*Alan beek,*" he said to Farrell, extending a hand, and to Mrs. Pollifax, "*As salam alaikum!*"

Mrs. Pollifax promptly replied, "*Alaikum as salam!*"

He looked pleased at this.

Mrs. Pollifax was relieved, seeing him. He had a natural dignity that was surprising in a sixteen-year-old; his dark face was very attractive, with a mouth that looked accustomed to smiling, and his dark eyes held warmth. She would have thought him older; she thought that above all he looked a happy young man, unlike so many American boys of his age.

"I brought you Hilweh," he told Hanan, "and camels for Youseff and your guests to take a small ride if they wish."

"Oh dear," murmured Mrs. Pollifax.

Farrell, amused, said, "I can't imagine anything that would make Mrs. Pollifax happier. How very thoughtful of you!"

Mrs. Pollifax gave him a reproachful glance.

"I brought only the gentlest camels," said Qasim, after a glance at her face, and he proceeded to introduce the four animals and describe their breeding, explaining that each winter for two months he went to the city to attend a government program on husbandry. "See? Very gentle."

It was in this manner that Mrs. Pollifax was introduced to her first camel. With a prod, the dun-colored one folded himself up so that she could—with Qasim's help—mount the creature and seat herself on the blanketed and gaily decorated saddle. Another prod from Qasim tipped her forward as the camel rose to his feet, and then sent her sliding back as he steadied himself. After this, with Qasim leading, she and the camel went for a lurching, amiable, and lazy stroll. He was much higher than a horse, but she found more to hold on to, and after being led around the camp, followed by a swarm of delighted children, she admitted that a camel was an improvement over a horse, and she would be willing to ride to the small hill that was half a mile away.

Farrell and Joseph mounted their camels with confidence, Qasim climbed on his horse, while Hanan shouted, "*Way-oh! Way-oh! Hei! Hei! Hei!*" and set off at a gallop on her white camel Hilweh, a name that she explained meant "beautiful."

They experienced only one moment of concern during their ride. From the east came the peculiar chatter of a helicopter churning the air with its blades, at first no more than a huge bird in the sky and of no consequence, but as it neared them, flying surprisingly low, the sound grew loud and sent Qasim's horse rearing in panic.

As Qasim steadied him, Farrell said, "Civilization! Do they often fly over like that?"

"No," said Qasim indignantly, staring at the receding helicopter. "If they did, my horse would not be frightened like this." Staring after it he said, "Who was it, Youseff, could you see? It wasn't the Desert Patrol, was it?"

Joseph shook his head. "Or the military. Too small. Maybe a government helicopter, but I saw no markings. Someone may be lost in the desert."

Qasim nodded. "Or looking for smugglers."

"Smugglers?" echoed Mrs. Pollifax.

Joseph nodded. "The Saudi border is only an hour or so away from us."

"That close!"

"Yes."

They watched the silver bird disappear into the horizon and continued their ride, and once over the hill they rode a mile farther to see the herds of sheep, and Mrs. Pollifax was content. The air was clear and the sun was hot, but not uncomfortably so, and she only wished that Cyrus could see her now. Certainly she felt pleased with herself after her previous ventures on a horse, but horses reminded her of Petra and of being attacked in the Siq, and she preferred not to think about that. Instead she chose to imagine Lawrence of Arabia riding over this same mile of the desert, because Jordan—Transjordan then—was where he had led the Arabs into battle.

When they returned from their excursion into the desert, it was obvious to Mrs. Pollifax that they would not be leaving for the buried fort, unless by night, for the camp was readying itself for the *mansef,* feast. A sheep was being roasted and turned on a spit, head and eyes intact, and she tried not to look at it—if only, she thought, it did not *look* like a sheep. Relaxing on pillows in the sheikh's tent, she and Farrell were at once brought the ubiquitous coffee by a young man, who inquired in very poor English if they had "employed a delicious *jamal* dribe." Farrell assured him gravely that yes, they had enjoyed it very much, and the young man went away, satisfied. The tent was now opened to the west, and they were given a spectacular view of the sun approaching the horizon, sending out flares of brilliant orange and gold, and as it reached the horizon Mrs. Pollifax touched Farrell's arm and said, "Look."

Off to their right Sheikh Ibn Jidoor had appeared, and after a glance at the sunset he carefully removed each of his sandals and sank to the ground in the position of prayer. A moment later he prostrated himself, forehead touching the earth, and repeated this twice before straightening, the last of the sun etching his profile in gold. It was a sight that moved Mrs. Pollifax; she supposed that all through the camp the men were on their knees in submission to Allah, but she did not turn her head to look. She merely sat very still: the silence of the desert, the sun, and the praying man she would not easily forget.

And then it was over, and the sheikh disappeared from sight. A chill invaded the tent, and the opened side was dropped, enclosing them in the fire-warmed tent with its smells of roasting meat, freshly brewed coffee, and mysterious herbs. Men began filtering in, sitting cross-legged in a circle around the fire, and more cups of coffee were distributed. The sheikh entered, to courteously greet each guest, and to introduce Mrs. Pollifax as Assayida Pollifax and Farrell as Assayed Farrell. Joseph came in and was cordially greeted and questioned in Arabic; there was laughter and a lighting of pipes and a warmth of cordiality.

And then came the feast . . . huge bowls heaped with rice and pieces of lamb dripping in oil, all to be eaten with the fingers, but mercifully there were no sheep's eyes. This was followed by cups of very sweet tea and serious talk.

Joseph, turning to Farrell and Mrs. Pollifax, translated what was being said. "They're talking about Hanan's wanting Awad to show you the buried fort tomorrow. My grandfather does not like this. Only a month ago one of my grandfather's men set off into the desert to track four missing goats. The goats he found, but he came upon a terrible sight: several men who had lost their way in the desert, one already dead from heat and thirst, the others close to death, but thanks be to Allah, now being slowly restored to life. My grandfather is asking how old Awad's truck is and in what condition. He has every respect for Awad, but the desert is cruel and you are his honored guests, your safety his responsibility."

"We are not to go, then?" said Farrell.

Joseph held up his hand, listening. "Ah, my grandfather says that first Argub al-Saidai must inspect Awad's pickup truck, he says Awad may know the desert like the palm of his hand, and he may know camels, but he does not know machines."

Mrs. Pollifax smiled. "Your grandfather worries like any good parent."

"And is very wise," added Joseph.

A flap of the tent opened and a young man entered, carrying what looked like a thin leather box on a pole. He was given warm and lengthy greetings, as if expected, and Joseph said, smiling, "Music. He will play for us on the rababa."

But Farrell had noticed the sky beyond the young man as he entered, and with a polite smile he rose, saying, "What stars I see! Excuse me but I'm going to see if I can find the Milky Way, and who knows, maybe the North Star."

"You *may* see a *shibah*—a falling star!" said Joseph. "Like a gift from Allah."

When he left Mrs. Pollifax felt a little lonely, a feeling that was not assuaged by the young musician who had joined them. Leaning over his instrument as if it were a Stradivarius, he strummed the one-stringed *rababa* and began to sing. It sounded a very melancholy song, and he sang it in a loud, slightly nasal voice. Joseph translated for her.

Love, love, in vain we count the days of
   Spring,
Lost is all love's pain, long the songs we
   sing.
Sunshine and summer rain, Winter and
   Spring again,
Still the years shall bring, but we die. . . .
His torch, love, the sun, turns to the stormy
   west,
Like a fair dream begun, changing to jest;
Love, while our souls are one, let us sing
   the sun,
Sing and forget the rest. . . . And so die.

Definitely melancholy, thought Mrs. Pollifax. A tray of sweets was being passed around, flaky pastries drenched in honey. *"Baqlawa,"* whispered Joseph, but the tent flap had opened again and Mrs. Pollifax looked up eagerly, hoping that Farrell had returned. Instead it was a Bedouin, heavily robed, who entered unobtrusively and joined them.

The sheikh tossed an added handful of dried dung on the fire and the sudden brightness more clearly illuminated the circle of faces around her. Across the fire she met the eyes of the man who had so quietly entered. He was staring at her, frowning and puzzled, and seeing this she looked at him more closely: a weathered face, swarthy in the firelight, black-browed and clean-shaven, but with strange patches of white skin on each cheekbone. Regarding him with equal interest she smiled politely before turning away, for the sheikh had been speaking to her. She said, "What? I'm so sorry," and watched as the stranger rose and walked out of the tent.

"From the Northeast," she replied when he repeated his question. "It is called Connecticut."

"Ah, Kenitcut." He nodded, smiling benevolently. "And now you are here."

"Yes—with Hanan, who is—a *real bedu*?"

He laughed, his teeth white and strong, and nodded his head vigorously, but she was growing impatient for Farrell to return, and it was warm in the tent. She wondered how gracefully she could rise after being seated cross-legged for so long, and so out of practice. Gingerly she grasped one leg and straightened it, easing the stiffness, and thus gaining leverage she said, "Please excuse me, I will see if Mr. Farrell has found a falling star," and managed to stand up without tottering.

Outside, the camp was very still, the sky a velvety ink blue and filled with stars, but there was no sign of Farrell. She walked in and among the tents, looking for him, and at last began to call out his name.

There was no answer.

When she reappeared in the sheikh's tent, it was to stand at its entrance and say in a loud voice that only barely concealed her panic, "*I cannot find Farrell!*"

The firelit faces of the men turned to her, not comprehending until Joseph stood up, translating her words into Arabic. At once Awad rose to his feet, followed by several of the men.

"What can have happened?" she demanded of Joseph.

"He walked too far," Joseph said. "We will find him. Bushaq, bring lanterns!"

Lanterns were produced, and the men separated, going in different directions, but Mrs. Pollifax stayed with Awad, who did not call out Farrell's name but studied the ground. She followed him as he slowly made his way to the northern end of the camp, his lantern held low.

"*Bismallah!*" he suddenly cried. "Look!"

Two other lanterns converged on his, and Mrs. Pollifax moved closer. The added streams of steady flame illuminated a swath of disturbed earth, a broad scar that extended beyond the light and disappeared into the darkness. Arabic words rose and fell around Mrs. Pollifax, but she needed no explanation. This was the mark of something or someone being dragged away into the darkness. Turning to Mrs. Pollifax, Awad said, "You see? You know?"

She nodded. "But why didn't he call out? Why didn't he scream?" she demanded, and realized that she was fighting back a scream of her own.

Awad didn't reply; to the others he spoke in Arabic, and the lights of the lanterns moved to follow the drag marks out into the darkness. Mrs. Pollifax followed automatically. . . . The lanterns, held low, traced the broad swath past the camp, up a slight incline, down, up, and in and through a cluster of sheep, and did not end until the flickering tent fires of the camp behind them were distant. Here the marks abruptly ended and Awad, kneeling, said, "*Horses.*"

"Horses!" cried out Mrs. Pollifax.

In the light of the lanterns the men's faces were fierce yet compassionate, wondering, eyes narrowed.

Awad's lantern combed the earth. "Two," he said. His lantern moved farther, and he plucked a dropping of dung from the ground. "See? Horses." He let it fall, his lantern closer to the ground, his shrewd eyes seeing details lost to Mrs.

Pollifax. "Two horses came from the east," he said, "both carrying one rider, the weight is same." He moved with his lantern again, the others watching and waiting. "Here, they rode away back east, but see? The prints of this horse are much heavier, carrying a load."

"Carrying Farrell," she whispered, nodding, and then she said aloud, despairingly, *"But why Farrell?"*

"Wait," said Awad sharply. "Bring more light, here is a patch of sand." And then, turning to Mrs. Pollifax, "Come see! Do you know this footprint—half a footprint— made as the man mounted his horse?"

She looked at it blankly, and then at Awad. He said, "This half print is known to me—and to you. It is made by the shoe of the man who stood at the door of my house last night and who stole Youseff's battery."

Bewildered, Mrs. Pollifax said, "But that cannot be! We thought—we were so sure it was the men in the red car who—" She stopped as they looked at her uncomprehendingly. How, she wondered, could she possibly explain that the men following them in the red sedan had been following *her,* not Farrell, and that she and Farrell had assumed it was those men who had visited the house in the night to disable both taxi and truck.

It should have been me, she thought. *Why didn't they take* me? There was an answer lurking in the back of her mind, but too fleeting to capture now in these moments of shock, when she felt only a desperate worry. "Where would they have taken him?" she asked Awad. "Can we go after them? They can't have gone far, please can we follow?"

He said bluntly, "Not until sunrise, we need light. Good light," and he added sternly, "This is grave insult, a matter of honor to Sheikh Ibn Jidoor. In his own camp!"

A small hand slid into Mrs. Pollifax's comfortingly; she had not noticed that Hanan was here. "Do not worry," Hanan whispered. "We will find him."

Mrs. Pollifax appreciated her confidence, but sunrise was seven hours away, and who could know what might happen to Farrell or how far away he would be by then?

Muttering puzzled, angry words, with a

number of calls upon Allah, the men stalked back to the camp, led by Awad. Mrs. Pollifax walked more slowly, hoping she need not speak to anyone again until sunrise. Hanan walked with her, and Mrs. Pollifax realized that if she wanted sleep now—and to her surprise it was ten o'clock by her watch—she would have to join and meet the women in the *muharram* behind the curtained half of the tent. She dreaded this but Hanan, as if she understood, entered and spoke in Arabic to the women, who made clucking sounds of sympathy, brought Mrs. Pollifax blankets, and gave her kind glances.

She lay down, aware that Hanan lay across from her under her own blanket. The sound of voices on the other side of the curtain gradually faded. . . . Her mind was in turmoil, worried and afraid for Farrell, but it had been a long day and after a nightmarish half hour she drifted into an uneasy sleep.

She was awakened by a hand gripping her arm. She heard Hanan whisper, "It's me. . . . Do not make a sound. Come!"

To ask for an explanation threatened to wake up the sleeping forms around her;

cautiously Mrs. Pollifax untangled herself from her blanket and crept outside after Hanan. In silence Hanan drew her away from the tents and, still whispering, said, "We can go now. Qasim will help us."

"Qasim?" echoed Mrs. Pollifax. "Go now?"

"Qasim has thought of a place where they may have taken Mr. Farrell."

Not quite awake yet, Mrs. Pollifax stammered, "But—w-w-where?"

She could see better now in the darkness; Hanan was considering this. "I think fifteen or twenty kilometers from here."

"But how will you find the tracks in the dark?"

Hanan smiled. "If one *knows* a place Mr. Farrell could be found, a person need not look for tracks, only follow the stars." She added almost scornfully, "Awad is too cautious."

Thoroughly awake now, Mrs. Pollifax regarded her with fascination. "And you and Qasim have decided this?"

"Oh yes," Hanan said confidently. "He has saddled three camels for us and is waiting not far away."

"Camels!"

Hanan nodded. "Yes, to steal Awad's truck would wake up everyone. One must agree, it is a very noisy truck."

"Hanan," said Mrs. Pollifax, half laughing, "you are incredible."

"But a person must *try,*" said Hanan. "We have a saying 'Seize a thief before he seizes you,' and Mr. Farrell has been stolen."

A dog barked and was stilled. Hanan led her away from the camp and toward the hill where Qasim was waiting in such a dark robe that he was no more than a shadow. The three camels beside him stirred restlessly.

"*Masal khair,*" Hanan said to him in a low voice.

"*Winta dkhair,*" he said gravely, and then, "Let's go!"

16

The night was cold, there was only a crescent moon that shed no light, but the stars glittered coldly in the sky like cut diamonds. There was no wind but Mrs. Pollifax shivered, whether from a chill or suspense she didn't know; she had begun to repeat to herself all that Farrell had belatedly told her about "others" possibly wanting Dib Assen's manuscript. There was the Iraqi agent who had been killed at the castle, of course. Now, in her mind, she arranged and rearranged the added events whose impact she had resisted: the man who had joined Farrell in the hotel dining room to speak of Arab literature and whom Farrell was sure he'd seen during the sandstorm, waiting outside the restaurant. . . . It was no longer Mr.

Nayef who mattered; he was relegated now to the status of a mere irritation, because all the time . . .

But still she couldn't quite grasp the reality of this. It was true that she'd accompanied Farrell to Jordan for an expected rendezvous with the friend of the late Dib Assen, but her attention had lately become so occupied by the dusty red sedan following them, and the attack on her at Petra, that to shift attention to Farrell's mysterious "others" short-circuited her concentration. Farrell had neither seen nor met Ibrahim, he didn't have the manuscript in his possession, yet he was gone, mysteriously vanished, dragged off into the night, when surely it ought to have been Emily Pollifax instead.

She shivered. They had been steadily plodding along in a silence broken only by the creak of saddle leather or the cough of a camel. With the camp far behind them now, Qasim called over his shoulder, "I think we head north of the Qasr and ride back to it through the Wadi Ghaduf. To not be seen or heard."

Behind her Hanan called back to him, "But the stones, Qasim! The stones in the

Wadi Ghaduf are so sharp they cut the feet of the camels, you know that."

"Yes and I have brought thick wool to pad their feet," he told her. "You must help me with this, both of you, or it will take too long."

"But where are we going?" pleaded Mrs. Pollifax.

He pulled back his camel to ride beside her. "To the ruins of an old castle. There are many in the north of Jordan, but this is the only one in this part of the desert."

"Not the half-buried fort!" she exclaimed.

He vigorously shook his head. "That is very far, and only Awad knows it. This one the Omayyads began to build nearly thirteen hundred years ago but never finished. It's called the Qasr at Tūba. Nobody goes there now. Except *bedu* maybe."

"And bats," added Hanan.

"But no others."

"And you think—?" asked Mrs. Pollifax.

Qasim turned in his saddle to look at her. He said fiercely, "It is the law of the *bedu* that even an enemy is safe in a *bedu* camp. For someone to steal a guest from the sheikh is a terrible insult. If they plan to ask much ransom—"

Ransom! Mrs. Pollifax could only hope it might be that simple.

"—they would not carry him across the border into Saudi Arabia, which is very near, because there is only empty desert. We think, Hanan and I, they would need a very clever place to hide. Not a tent, where no tent has been seen before—that would be noticed—but maybe the forgotten ruins of the Qasr at Tūba, which has stood there forever. That would be clever—for a little while—and there is still a roof. We will see, *na'am*?"

Thinking about this Mrs. Pollifax said, "But whoever did this would have to know the desert very well."

Qasim said flatly, "He would not— *could* not—be *bedu.*"

"No," agreed Mrs. Pollifax softly.

Hanan, behind them, said, "Stop—listen!"

Mrs. Pollifax did not know how to stop a camel, but Qasim reached over and accomplished this for her. They waited, listening.

"A plane," Hanan said.

Qasim nodded. In the clear desert night air they could hear the faint drone of a plane in the distance and see its lights until it disappeared, turning north.

"I do not understand," said Hanan. "Two in one day?"

"At least they didn't see us," pointed out Mrs. Pollifax.

"No."

They resumed their steady pace, side by side now. The sky overhead was like a rich blue tapestry knit with stars, a description that Mrs. Pollifax felt was very apt for a sky that had seen ancient kings, soldiers, nomads, explorers, and adventurers pass below it. With the plane gone the silence enfolded them again like a blanket. The desert was changed at night, she realized, there was no detail, only the earth and sky between which they rode, very tiny in the scale of things, and very mortal. "Is it much farther?" she asked.

Hanan had turned in her saddle to look behind them.

"What is it? Did you drop something?"

Hanan shook her head. "It was nothing," she said, but Qasim gave her a curious glance. To Mrs. Pollifax he said, "We turn north now to the Wadi Ghaduf, which is not far. If it was sunrise the castle could be seen from here, but we must not go straight to it. The wadi has steep walls to hide us." Again Hanan had turned to look behind them, and Qasim added sharply, "What *is* it, Hanan?"

Hanan said uneasily, "Nothing, really."

"You think someone is behind us?"

"I don't know, Qasim, it's just a feeling, a strange feeling in my *'alb*—my heart," she added politely for Mrs. Pollifax.

"We will go faster," said Qasim, nodding. "We need the wadi."

The faster pace jolted Mrs. Pollifax enough to keep her alert, but she was growing tired, having had no sleep this night except for the few minutes before Hanan had awakened her. She wondered what was happening to Farrell now. . . . She wondered if they would have to return empty-handed to the camp before the night ended. . . . In the meantime she felt welded to her camel and increasingly uncomfortable, the rhythmic swaying of her camel inducing drowsiness. She yawned a few times.

Abruptly Qasim stopped. "We are here.

Deer balak! Be careful!'' He dismounted and led Mrs. Pollifax's camel down a steep incline into what felt like a pit; it was instead a dried-up streambed, quite deep and wide, its walls furred with grass.

Once all three camels were in the wadi, Qasim unstrapped his saddlebag. He brought out squares of cloth and shreds of rope, and Mrs. Pollifax was at last able to contribute something: her small pocket flashlight. Shielding the light they wrapped the feet of each camel, but only after Qasim had bound their jaws with strips of cloth so they wouldn't howl in protest, belch noisily, or bray. They mounted again, slowly moving uphill, so that Mrs. Pollifax slid back and forth in the saddle as they rode toward the plateau ahead.

Suddenly Qasim halted, and they nearly ran into him. "*Intabeh*—look!'' he said, pointing. "*Kneek!*''

A massive shape loomed ahead of them at the peak of the incline, solid and substantial and darker than the night sky. Its great roof was arched, its walls full of empty shapes through which she could see the stars, but the light shining from one of its cavities was not a star, it was the yellow light of a lantern shining inside.

People were there.

Bedouins camping for the night, wondered Mrs. Pollifax, *or Farrell*? and then, "Now what?"

"We tie the camels here," Qasim said calmly.

Hanan whispered, "We must go to the dark west end, farthest from the light." And to Mrs. Pollifax, "That big arched roof was made to be a great hall for *mansef,* feasts."

Qasim had couched the animals, threading the ropes from their nose rings around the largest stones he could find to secure them. After this they crept closer, with Qasim in the lead; the wadi widened and came to an end, leaving them suddenly exposed. Furtively they made their way across the level ground to the dark end of the building. Through gaps in the broken wall they entered a ghostly room with no roof, its floor cluttered with fallen bricks and stone. There were no sounds, no voices, only the flutter of a bat's wings above them, and then silence again. Qasim pointed to an arched doorway, still intact, and they picked their way across the shards to peer beyond it.

They were looking into the great arch-roofed banquet hall, open to the desert at one end, but the hall was not empty: it was occupied by a large shape, which even in the darkness gleamed silver. Tracing the outline of it with her eyes Mrs. Pollifax drew in her breath sharply; beside her, she heard both Hanan and Qasim gasp.

"The helicopter!" breathed Hanan.

Mrs. Pollifax felt distinctly chilled by this, realizing that if Farrell was here this was certainly a well-organized abduction. The helicopter would have had no trouble landing on the level ground of the plateau outside, and was small enough to have been taxied inside, out of sight, without damage to its blades.

"Farrell *has* to be here," she whispered. For what other purpose would a private helicopter have been flown here, certainly not for a meeting of corporate executives in the middle of a desert. He had to be here, and they had to get him out.

"Let's look," she said.

"Look?" repeated Qasim.

"At what?" asked Hanan.

She did not take time to explain. She had once, in a desperate situation in Turkey, herded friends into just such a helicopter, and without the slightest knowledge of how to make it fly she had managed to get it off the ground. Not far *enough* off the ground, but it had flown them out of danger until it ran out of gas and landed them in a city's busy marketplace, scattering people like chickens.

She said only, "It could be useful."

If there had been a hatch door, it had been removed. She climbed into the cockpit, sat down in the pilot's seat, and turned on her pocket flashlight.

"*Bismallah!* For what do you search?" whispered a startled Qasim, peering inside and watching the tiny circle of light examine the interior.

"Levers," she said. "There should be two."

Her light moved down, illuminating a lever that jutted up from the floor, and she smiled; moving the light, she discovered the lever that extended out from behind the seat and nodded, remembering. Climbing out to join an astonished Hanan and Qasim, she remained doubtful—one could not, after all, risk moving the up lever by mistake and hitting the roof—but there was possibility here. She knew the importance of possibility, because once, living without it, and before she met Carstairs, she had almost stepped off the roof of her apartment building when tending her geraniums.

"You know how to fly this?" whispered Qasim, as she climbed down to join them.

She said vaguely, "One could, I suppose, it's not locked, the key's there. . . . But enough! What now?"

Qasim led them around the helicopter toward the opposite wall of the banquet hall; they climbed over more shards, crossed a narrow roofless corridor open to the stars, and now they could see a flicker of light ahead, emanating from what had once been a proper doorway until falling rocks had tumbled across it, reducing it to half an entrance.

But they had found the Lantern Room.

"There is that window, too," whispered Hanan. "The window we saw from the wadi, showing light. We could look through that."

Mrs. Pollifax shook her head. "They might see us, windows can be dangerous. Let's listen first, listen for voices and see how many there are."

A voice was suddenly heard raised in anger, followed by a sharp *crack*! Mrs. Pollifax knew that sound—she still wore the scars of it across her back—and she was sickened by it, as she realized what they were doing to Farrell to make him speak.

He spoke now. He shouted, "I don't *have* it, I tell you!"

A new voice murmured something, and Mrs. Pollifax held up two fingers. "Two men."

Qasim tugged at her arm. "We must *talk,*" he whispered.

They retreated to the banquet hall where they could talk in low voices, without whispering.

Hanan said solemnly, "They are hurting Mr. Farrell, aren't they?"

"Yes," said Mrs. Pollifax.

"Do they have guns?"

"Little cousin," said Qasim, "such men always have guns. We must *think* now. Two men, Mrs. Pollifax?"

"I think so, yes," she said. "One man with a whip, one to give orders, but there could be more."

Hanan said impatiently, "If we could only make them come *out.* If we could make noises they would come out, wouldn't they?"

Qasim said, "What noise could bring them out, Hanan, a scream, a shout, and what then? I do not know why they do this to Mr. Farrell, but men who have helicopters are clever and rich."

"Helicopter," mused Mrs. Pollifax, and she lifted her gaze to the machine looming above them. "The noise of the helicopter could certainly bring out *someone,*" she said. "And I think they would come through that door, which is only half blocked, because it's nearest the plane."

Hanan said eagerly, "And I could stand on a pile of rocks by that door, and as they come out I could hit them over the head! Oh please see if you can do it, Mrs. Pollifax!"

"You think you could start the engine?" asked Qasim.

"Let me try," she told him. "Help me up

into the cockpit, Qasim, and Hanan—collect your rocks."

She climbed again into the helicopter and turned on her pocket flashlight. Taking care to avoid touching a lever by mistake, she turned the only key that she saw, and then began pressing what movable protuberances she could find: this was promising because the engine stirred, sputtered, and then roared. Unfortunately the blades began turning overhead, too, but since she was helpless to stop their whirring she climbed out to learn what this accomplished.

She found Qasim and Hanan poised like statues on either side of the doorway, rocks in hand. It needed a minute before they heard the clatter of stones as a man groped for a foothold; a head appeared, and once the man cleared the rocks, he placed both feet on the ground, and at once Qasim hit him with a rock and he fell flat.

"Now there is only one man inside," said Qasim in a pleased voice.

"La," said a voice behind them, "there is me—Faisel!" The three of them whirled to find that a man had crept up behind them, carrying under one arm an ugly shape that in the darkness looked very much like a submachine gun. *He must have been on guard,* she realized, shocked by their lack of foresight, *but where did he come from, how did we miss him, was he asleep? Where did he come from?*

"Damn!" she said loudly and furiously.

"In," he told them, pointing to the rock-strewn doorway, " *'ajjel!'* "

Since the man, *Faisel,* appeared to have no concern for the prostrate man on the ground, Mrs. Pollifax stepped over him with an equal lack of concern. Finding a toehold among the rocks she climbed over them and half fell, half jumped down into the lit room, Hanan behind her, followed by Qasim, followed by Faisel.

Standing just inside the room Mrs. Pollifax thought for a moment that she had stepped back in time and was looking at a tableau in chiaroscuro—a study in light and shadow—labeled "*Scene from Ancient Arabia, Fifteenth Century.*" This was because her sudden entry had frozen all movement and she saw that she had misjudged the occupants of the room: there were two of them standing, both posed theatrically in elegant striped robes and *kaffiyehs* with daggers in their belts, one of them with a whip, the other holding a pistol. Each of them was half shadowed by the light of the lantern, which shone with the brilliance of a gold coin, etching clearly every stone in the ancient wall above and lightly brushing the faces of the two men staring at her before the gold faded into the darkness beyond them.

And then abruptly the tableau ended and she was returned to the twentieth century; the two men came to life, and the third man, who lay on the floor spread-eagled and stripped to the waist, turned his head with difficulty to say wearily, *"Et tu,* Duchess?"

17

If it was nearing midnight in Jordan, it was late afternoon in Langley, Virginia, and Carstairs was at his desk and growing impatient. He had a direct line to the CIA office in Amman, and he had been in communication with Hugh Rawlings off and on during the day. Now he sat with a cup of coffee and attempted to put together the fragments of news that he had received from Rawlings at various hours, none of them satisfying.

Rawlings, he thought, was growing frantic. Intelligence in Jordan resisted sharing information with another country whose aid they accepted, a dependency that rendered them suspect in their neighboring Arab countries. A matter of pride, of course, and quite understandable, but

Rawlings was being given only snatches of news and much of it contradictory.

In his first call of the day, Rawlings said he'd learned from the police that Mrs. Pollifax and Farrell had not returned to their hotel when expected, and that Jidoor Tours was being contacted to learn where their guide had taken them.

On the other hand, an hour later, Rawlings had been told by Intelligence that everything was under complete control, the mysterious key had been identified by Palace Security—any mention of what door or safe it would unlock was top secret, of course—and precautions were being taken to protect whatever it gave access to, and the map or diagram was being analyzed by experts to uncover Slaman's plans for October 30. Intelligence had assured Rawlings that all was well.

A third phone call from a frustrated Rawlings reported that, according to the police, the family of one Youseff Jidoor had been visited, and he had been surprised to learn that Jidoor Tours was only a one-man operation. However, the guide's mother had known exactly where

Youseff was taking his clients: they had headed south to the desert to visit Youseff's grandfather, who was a sheikh. The police, Rawlings had continued, were organizing a search to find out just where the sheikh and his camp were located this month in the desert. Fortune had briefly smiled on them when they'd realized that a young member of the Criminal Investigation Department named Mifleh Jidoor was brother to Youseff, or Joseph, and might pinpoint more precisely where to find the grandfather, but unfortunately they'd not been able to find him yet.

The last call from Rawlings had sounded discouraged. "I've reached Intelligence again," he said. "They were more forthcoming this time. Nobody knows where Suhair Slaman is—he's certainly not in Amsterdam—but they're investigating reports that several men slipped across the Syrian border two nights ago, they were spotted by a family of Bedouins." He added indignantly, "In spite of that stepped-up border patrol, too!"

"It's a long border," pointed out Carstairs. "What about the red sedan that

was glued to Mrs. Pollifax and Farrell for
several days?"

Rawlings had sighed heavily. "Who
knows? The police waited for Mrs. Pollifax's return to Amman so they could
move in on the men keeping her under
surveillance, but she didn't return. Those
men are probably the only people in Jordan who know where she is, damn it."

"So where does it stand now?" Carstairs had asked him.

"I'm trying to sort it all out," growled
Rawlings. "It's dark now, and how the hell
they can search for anyone at night—and
in a desert—I don't know. It's a big desert."

Seated now over his cup of coffee, Carstairs tried to sum up matters for himself.
He decided (1) that Suhair Slaman and a
few select hit men were probably in Jordan now, prepared to establish themselves in place for whatever was planned
for October 30, quite possibly another attempt at assassinating the king; (2) that
Farrell and Mrs. Pollifax were in the desert
visiting a sheikh, and if they'd left Amman,
it meant that either Farrell had success-
fully met with Ibrahim, or had *not* met with

him and had given up hope; and (3) that if neither the police nor Intelligence had found the sheikh's camp yet, it was not likely that anyone else could have found them in the dark.

Except, he realized, frowning, for the men in the red sedan. On the other hand, he had flown over enough deserts to know that in general they were tediously flat, with a visibility that extended for miles, except during a sandstorm. Surely no one in that red sedan would be fool-hardy enough to openly follow Mrs. Pollifax and Farrell to the sheikh's camp, and this implied that everyone, himself in-cluded, could relax now.

But could they?

Carstairs sat back in his chair, frowning. Bishop, bringing in a sheaf of papers for him to sign, said, "You look full of gloom and doom, what's wrong?"

"I don't know," Carstairs told him, frowning. "It's just a feeling that's begun haunting me."

"About what or whom?"

"It's Mrs. Pollifax and Farrell," he ad-mitted reluctantly. "You heard Rawlings's disjointed reports today. I would very

much like to envision Mrs. Pollifax's delight in meeting a real-life sheikh, but I
don't feel comfortable about this. For instance, what the hell are the two of them
doing in the desert, are they escaping
someone or something, or simply on
tour? If Farrell had met with this man
Ibrahim and secured the manuscript, do
you really think he'd carry it around with
him and go off on holiday to the desert
with it?"

"It doesn't sound like Farrell," agreed
Bishop, pulling up a chair and seating
himself.

"Damn unlikely," growled Carstairs.
"He'd book the first available flight out of
Amman."

"But we do know that he and Mrs. Pollifax spent mornings at Karak castle, and
it's possible—"

"Yes, at Karak castle," said Carstairs.
"Where Mrs. Pollifax found a dead Iraqi in
a closet or whatever, and where the main
suspect who rushed away from the scene
that morning *could* have been Ibrahim.
Consider how interested the Iraqis must
be now in Farrell and Mrs. Pollifax, who
just happened to be at the castle at the

time! Especially if they'd been tailing Ibrahim."

"If it *was* Ibrahim," pointed out Bishop. "A lot of ifs and could bes there, you know."

"We deal in ifs and could bes," Carstairs reminded him curtly. "It also irritates me to keep referring to the car following Mrs. Pollifax and Farrell as just a red sedan. It's a hell of a lot more than that; it's a red sedan following them on the orders of a terrorist. In a word, it's Suhair Slaman personally keeping an eye on Mrs. Pollifax."

"Yes, but—"

"And if," interrupted Carstairs, "the Iraqis should be obsessed with finding Ibrahim—"

"*If* it was Ibrahim," Bishop put in, and ducked Carstairs's reproachful glance. "Sorry, sir."

"—then they know about Dib Assen's manuscript, they want it, they know about Farrell now, or at the very least suspect him—"

Bishop winced. "I see what you mean. You're worried."

"Thank you, Bishop," said Carstairs,

with exaggerated politeness, "I'm delighted and relieved that you finally understand. And yes, you're damn right I'm
concerned, and it's a sudden feeling
that's not going away."

"One of your psychic flashes," said
Bishop, nodding.

"That sounds damnably flippant," Carstairs told him. "Try imagining what a terrorist like Suhair Slaman would like to do
to Mrs. Pollifax if he catches up with her."

"Now *that's* hitting below the belt,"
Bishop told him indignantly.

"Then think what the Iraqis would like
to do with Farrell if they know why he's in
Jordan."

Bishop looked shaken. "You're really
serious, then. I apologize. You think that's
why they've headed for the desert—to
hide?"

"I've no idea why they went there,"
Carstairs said crossly, "but when they left
they were presumably still followed by
Suhair Slaman's men."

"But the police in Amman—" began
Bishop.

"The police in Amman," said Carstairs,
"know nothing about Ibrahim."

Bishop said helplessly, "No, I suppose not, but—" He stopped. "What are you afraid of?"

"What I am afraid of is that Farrell has *not* connected with Ibrahim and doesn't have the manuscript, and beginning with that assumption—"

"Oh God," said Bishop, "you mean we've got *all* of them after Farrell and Mrs. Pollifax? Both? Two groups? What can you do?"

Carstairs was silent, idly tapping his pencil on his desk while he thought. Abruptly he reached a decision. "I see only one thing I can do, and it's a feeble try at that. Put me through to Rawlings— on the double, before he leaves his office to go home to bed."

Five minutes later, the connection made, he was saying, "Rawlings, it's time I share a bit of information with you about John Sebastian Farrell and Emily Pollifax, who are *not* in Jordan on any assignment from me, but who have both done a hell of a lot of good work for us—*valuable* work. I want nothing to happen to them, you un- derstand me? Forget the Iraqis and Suhair Slaman, let the police deal with them. I want those two found, protected, and sent back to me in one piece."

He hung up before Rawlings could utter so much as a protest or ask a question.

Bishop, puzzled, said, "But he has no experience in this sort of thing. What can he do?"

"He's young—they're *all* young," Carstairs said cynically. "They sit behind their desks and collate data and make phone calls, grow smug and feel important. If I've scared him enough, he just may forego his eight hours of sleep in his comfortable bed in his air-conditioned apartment and head out for the desert and *find* them." He added dryly, "It's also possible that he'll get lost in the desert and have to be picked up by the Desert Patrol tomorrow, but at the very least he'll experience what is called reality in this business. It will be a learning experience for him."

18

Mrs. Pollifax, confronted with this scene of medieval horror, swallowed her anger and her pity for Farrell; she had no choice. Her glance moved from him to the man staring at her with blazing eyes, and even in his robe and *kaffiyeh* she recognized him; he was no longer in a black silk suit, but as his robe caught the light she saw from its sheen that he was still wearing silk.

"How did you get here?" he demanded, and to Faisel, "Turn off that engine—*'ajjel*!"

"He's telling you the truth," she told him in a loud voice. "Farrell doesn't *have* what you want!" Behind her Hanan and Qasim moved to her side, and she was touched by this move to support and to protect.

Farrell shouted, "For God's sake, Duchess, get out while you can—run!" and then seeing Hanan and Qasim, he groaned, "Oh *no!*"

"Not without you," she told him, and to the man in the silk robe, "We've met before; you were talking literature with Farrell in the hotel dining room. Presumably you have a name?"

He said mockingly, "Taimour will do since it is not my name. So . . . you are his accomplice, it seems. How accommodating of you to come looking for him, we have two of you now." To Qasim he said, *"Sit."*

Neither Hanan nor Qasim obeyed him.

"Meen haditha?" asked the man with the whip.

"She is his friend," Taimour explained.

"Ah!" The man raised his whip, and Mrs. Pollifax winced as he struck Farrell's bare back, leaving behind still another angry red stripe.

"Two of us to torture?" she said mockingly, moving closer to him. "And perhaps a child as well? Farrell can tell you nothing, he doesn't have what you want, and that's the truth."

"Of course he has it," snapped Taimour. "Do you think we have not read the police reports? You were at Karak castle. The man carrying the manuscript ran past you—of course he slipped it to this Farrell as he passed him, do you think we are idiots? You were both there to meet the man Ibrahim, were you not? And you met."

"We did *not* meet," she flung at him angrily. "That man was frightened, he rushed away, he was hurt."

"Then where is he now? You made no move to find him after he 'disappeared,' as you say?"

Not giant steps forward, thought Mrs. Pollifax, remembering a childhood game, *just scissor steps,* and as if determined to make him understand, she took two small steps closer to him. "Where could we look?" she demanded of him. "The man was to come to Karak castle, you already know that, but how could he return after what happened?"

He said impatiently, "I ask again— where is the manuscript?"

Two more scissor steps . . . "And I tell you again that we don't have it. . . . I don't have it, and Mr. Farrell doesn't have it."

He glanced down at the pistol he held in his hand, and then turned and said to his companion, "Tie her up, Zaid. If this Farrell won't talk, then *she* will, and if she refuses, then you can practice your whip on *her* and let her friends watch *that.*"

He deserved no mercy, and she was close enough now. The man with the whip—Zaid, he'd called him—had placed it on the ground, and from the folds of his robe he drew out a coil of rope. There was no suspicion in Taimour's face, and he was the important one; to him she was only a foolish woman, she supposed, and she drew a deep breath and positioned herself. *Make this count, Emily,* she told herself grimly, *there are no margins for error here,* and with a hard kick to his knee she struck out with her right hand at Taimour's throat, a merciless strike but she could not be sorry.

He staggered backward; the pistol fell from his hand, but as he sank to the floor the pistol exploded and she reeled from the impact of the bullet that punctured her left arm. "Qasim," she cried out, "the whip!"

Zaid was still gaping in astonishment at the fallen Taimour. Qasim leaped for the whip, snatching away not only the whip but the rope. "I will tie *him* up. Never," he gasped, "never have I met such evil men!"

"And may you never again," said Mrs. Pollifax, feeling suddenly weak.

"She's been shot!" cried Hanan, and running to Taimour she began tearing strips from his elegant silk robe to stem the bleeding.

"Shot?" Mrs. Pollifax said, surprised, and looked down at her arm to see rather a lot of blood dripping from it to the floor.

"Shot?" echoed Farrell, and struggled to stand up, one hand on his back and wincing at the touch. "Is it bad? Let me see."

Hanan regarded him with disapproval. "You must be *still*—I wrap you next."

"Flesh wound," Farrell said, peering at it with narrowed eyes. "They bleed like hell and hurt, but it doesn't look deep. Get the bleeding stopped!"

"The helicopter," Mrs. Pollifax said suddenly. "The engine's stopped—stopped ages ago, where is whatshisname—Faisel?"

A voice from the window said, "If you mean the fool we have rendered unconscious you need not look for him, we have taken care of him."

Hanan dropped the bandage she had readied for Mrs. Pollifax, Qasim stopped tying up Zaid, Farrell abruptly sat down, and Mrs. Pollifax stared in astonishment at the man climbing in through the window.

"Mr. Nayef?" she faltered.

"We meet again, Mrs. Pollifax," he said charmingly. "Hardar, come in," he told the man behind him, and looking around the room he said distastefully, "I do not know who all these people are but you and I need to talk."

"Talk," repeated Mrs. Pollifax. "But we need help, not talk. My friend Mr. Farrell has been hurt and—"

"I said *talk,*" he repeated harshly, no longer charming at all.

His man Hardar was climbing through the window now with a gun in his hand.

"Talk," she repeated, dazed by this new development and hugging her bleeding arm.

"I put a wooden plaque in your bag, as you must be aware by now. It has been difficult, recovering it, and we grow tired of playing games. You will please tell me where it can be found, or—"

"Or what?" demanded Qasim, moving toward him threateningly. "Who are you?"

Hardar waved his gun dramatically, and Mrs. Pollifax, distinctly light-headed by now, thought that tragedy was rapidly turning into farce. She didn't know whether to laugh or to cry and hoped she wasn't going to become hysterical. It was the window, she decided: all that was missing was a curtain and the entrance of Hamlet. This castle was not Elsinore, but it was dark and old, full of bats, and men did seem to keep coming through the window.

"His name is Nayef," she told Qasim, fighting back dizziness. "He wants his Urn Tomb." Pulling herself together, she made an effort to play for time, although she had no idea why. "How did *you* know we were here, Mr. Nayef?" she asked.

He looked amused. "Playing for time, Mrs. Pollifax? You are quite helpless, I assure you. Did you think we could for a moment lose sight of you? We have kept an eye on you—if from a distance and with a telescope. It is unfortunate that you chose to leave in the middle of the night. Hardar, however, is excellent at tracking, and we followed you. But let us begin at the beginning: where was the plaque when we searched your room?"

"In the knapsack," she said.

"Ah yes, the knapsack. But we have the knapsack now, it has been removed from your room at the hotel, and it is not in the knapsack."

Farrell said wearily, "Oh tell him, Duchess. All he can do is kill you."

"That's a very negative attitude, Farrell," she told him, and rallied to say, "The plaque, Mr. Nayef, is under the pillow in Mr. Farrell's room, number 308."

She had made him angry. She had paid no attention to the dagger he wore in his broad belt; now he walked toward her until they were eye to eye, the dagger in his hand. It was a splendid dagger, studded with turquoise, and it looked as if it had killed many people already.

He said softly, "The plaque is not under the pillow in Mr. Farrell's room, for that is a foolish place to hide anything, and it was the first place we looked when we searched *his* room." He pressed the point of the dagger against her neck. "Speak, or I will draw this slowly—very slowly—across your throat and you will die."

"The police have the plaque," she said.

Startled, he said, "And why should the police have it?" He pressed the dagger harder into her flesh. "*What do you know about my plaque?* Why should the police have it? Tell me!"

"Because," she began.

"I can answer that," said a voice from the window.

The window again. *"Hamlet,"* breathed Mrs. Pollifax.

"Drop the dagger, Slaman, or I'll gladly shoot you in the back," said Inspector Jafer, climbing through the window, and abruptly the room was filled with men in uniform, all armed.

How popular we are—and so suddenly,

thought Mrs. Pollifax, and reacted to this new assault on her nerves by fainting. It was the practical Hanan who calmly broke her fall to the stone floor.

19

When she opened her eyes Mrs. Pollifax discovered that she was no longer in the small lit room in the castle but had been carried outside into the fresh cold night air. A campfire had been kindled nearby, and Inspector Jafer and Farrell were seated next to it, drinking coffee and talking. She saw only half of them because a young man in uniform was leaning over her, frowning as he applied something to her left arm that stung.

"Ouch," she said.

He glanced up and smiled, said a few words in his own language, and after wrapping her arm in a fresh bandage of Taimour's striped silk, he tucked a blanket securely around her and departed. Following him with her eyes she saw that both the banquet hall and the helicopter were illuminated by a battery-powered spotlight so bright that it dimmed the stars overhead. Her attention returned to the fire and to the two men seated by it. She saw that Inspector Jafer was taking notes and asking questions of Farrell.

Which should be interesting, she thought dryly.

"The helicopter," Jafer was saying, "is registered in the name of a well-known official at the Iraqi embassy. Of course the most curious part of your abduction is . . ." He rather dramatically paused before saying with emphasis, "why *you*?"

Indeed yes, thought Mrs. Pollifax, and wondered how open Farrell could afford to be. He had a proprietary interest in Dib Assen's manuscript, as did Carstairs, too, apparently; he would not want to share it, and she could foresee all kinds of entanglements if his relief in surviving this night left him too confiding. Then she scolded herself for such a thought, as she remembered her past experiences with Farrell and his clear-headedness in moments of total chaos and of physical pain.

He was saying now, with a frown, "It's

hard for me to understand, too, Inspector. This man who called himself Taimour first approached me in Amman. That was our only previous encounter."

"In Amman!"

Farrell nodded. "Yes, in the hotel dining room. He walked over to my table, didn't introduce himself, asked if I was American, and then sat down to lecture me on Arabic literature."

"Literature?"

"Yes. With quite a few references to one particular Iraqi author. Do you read, Inspector?"

Jafer looked affronted. "Of course I read."

"Then perhaps you're familiar with the novels of Dib Assen?"

"But yes," Jafer said, startled. "And what has that to do with you?"

Farrell's voice sounded tired, and she wondered if the nice young man had treated his wounds yet. "I met Dib Assen years ago, in the United States, and we became good friends. This man Taimour appeared to know that we'd been friends; I suppose they kept files on everyone he said hello to. Once I admitted to this friendship and expressed my sadness at Assen's death, his questions grew more pointed."

Well done so far, thought Mrs. Pollifax, *if only a few words of it true;* she waited with curiosity for more.

"Go on," said Jafer.

Farrell sighed. "He seemed to think I was in Jordan to be given something— perhaps old journals of Assen's—something to keep his name alive, perhaps. That's what he rather jovially hinted, watching closely for my reaction. It was all quite tiresome. Fortunately Mrs. Pollifax arrived to join me, and I was probably a bit rude, getting rid of him, but I certainly didn't expect *this.*"

"And *were* you in Jordan to be given journals of your friend?" asked Jafer quickly.

Farrell's reply was fervent. "I would like to have been given *anything* of Dib Assen's—a journal, a letter, a ring, a token, a message—but I can assure you I have nothing of his. Unfortunately."

An adroit reply, thought Mrs. Pollifax, and certainly truthful, but one that neatly avoided Jafer's real question as to whether he had come to Jordan with such expectations. She saw Inspector Jafer smile faintly, open his mouth to speak, and then close it. He too had found this an interesting reply and was not for a moment fooled, she decided; the inspector was remembering those mornings at Karak castle, but he was apparently prepared to overlook Farrell's ingenuous reply.

Farrell changed the subject by saying pleasantly, "*I* was knocked over the head and carried here, but how on earth did *you* get here?"

"Not easily," murmured the inspector. "We've been looking for this Mr. Nayef ever since you turned over to us the plaque with its key and map. We've since learned that several men crossed the border from Syria into the desert two nights ago, and we suspected he could be one of them. Until then we were particularly interested in the men following you in that red sedan, except you left for the day and didn't come back to Amman, and neither did the men in the red car." He shrugged. "After interviewing Joseph's mother we were told that you'd left for the desert, and she explained—roughly—how we might find the sheikh's camp."

"Like a needle in a haystack, isn't it?" said Farrell. "Damn big desert!"

"Yes, but my men did reach the camp, only to find it in an uproar; it was reported back to me in Amman by portable telephone that you, Mr. Farrell, had been dragged away, and that Mrs. Pollifax and two young friends had left to find you. That's when I ordered a plane."

"A plane?" repeated Farrell.

"A plane, yes. We took off from Amman at once, with night-vision goggles and searchlight to look for movement in the desert. Unfortunately we saw nothing and—again unfortunately—we landed at a point some twelve kilometers away, closer to the Saudi border."

Mrs. Pollifax remembered that plane.

"It was Joseph's brother, Mifleh, who told us of the Qasr at Tūba." He made a face. "We decided it wouldn't be safe to fly the plane back here in the dark—too many wadis crisscrossing the desert to risk a landing. We had to walk—a forced march. Took time—too *much* time."

He looked around him. "Lonely place,

isn't it? I had no idea it existed, Amman being my governate. Very good thing we brought young Mifleh with us. A Bedouin, you know."

"Bedu?" said Farrell, with a smile.

"Yes, *bedu.* Very promising young man." He stared out into the night thoughtfully. "It's two hours to sunrise, but it should be light enough soon to see where a plane can land here." He called out, "Lieutenant Shakir?"

A young man appeared out of the darkness. "Sir?"

"I think you can begin the walk back to the plane now, Lieutenant Ghaith can fly the helicopter out. Somewhere out there—" He gestured expressively with his hands. "—there has to be a place to safely land. Take no chances, we want our prisoner behind bars as soon as possible."

"Yes, sir."

"Take Ayad with you—and flashlights!"

"Yes, sir!"

Mrs. Pollifax decided it was time to sit up and make her presence known. "We saw that plane," she told him, "but it was far away from us."

He smiled at her. "*Taib!* You are better! A pity we didn't see you from the plane, we could have spared you some of this—this carnage. And it is time, I think—the right moment—to tell you, Mrs. Pollifax, what you deserve to know about your Mr. Nayef. You do not, of course, travel in any circles that would acquaint you with terrorists."

"No," said Farrell, with a mischievous smile.

"No indeed," echoed Mrs. Pollifax primly.

"I am sorry to tell you that Mr. Nayef is *not* Mr. Nayef. He is only too well known to us—and to your CIA as well. His real name is Suhair Slaman. His militants were involved in a previous assassination attempt on our king, and the discovery of this key and its map, with the date of October 30 included, has left us very sure that another attempt is—*was*—planned."

"Good heavens," said Mrs. Pollifax.

He nodded. "Considering our suspicion that he was one of the men who crossed the border from Syria two nights ago, that key was desperately needed. Too valuable to mail, immediate delivery apparently necessary, impossible for him to fly into Amman . . . he took a chance on you.''

"What did the key unlock?'' she asked curiously.

Jafer laughed. "Even my chief won't be told *that.* Only Palace Security knows, and probably the director of Intelligence, but it was important enough to kill a man to secure it. The entire affair will be hushed up, of course, but if not for you, Mrs. Pollifax, and your surprising suspicion of that plaque, and its so conveniently breaking open—'' He paused, waiting, but neither Farrell nor Mrs. Pollifax cared to enlighten him; already he guessed too much.

"So we actually met a real terrorist,'' breathed Mrs. Pollifax. "Think of that, Farrell!''

"I'll think of it later,'' he told her with a grin.

Looking around her, Mrs. Pollifax asked, "But where is everyone?''

Jafer shrugged. "Two of my men are preparing the Iraqi you call Taimour for his trip on the helicopter. He's badly hurt.'' He looked at Mrs. Pollifax appraisingly.

"One wonders," he said, "with Mr. Farrell incapacitated, just who had such a keen knowledge of karate."

This too had to be ignored. "Will he be all right?" she asked.

"Eventually yes, but he will be flown out in a few minutes in the helicopter to the nearest military hospital. It is his helicopter, after all." He sighed. "Iraq could make life difficult if one of its people is not treated—" He snapped two fingers together. "It will be difficult enough explaining how he—" He stopped, and Mrs. Pollifax smiled politely.

"—was not at all likable," she agreed.

"That I can imagine, yes. A hard trip for him, a tight fit, but we must get him out. His two companions will go in the plane. Unsavory brutes, both of them, but they will be suitable company for your Mr. Nayef—Suhair Slaman—who will be delivered to prison as soon as Lieutenant Shakir flies in."

"But Hanan," said Mrs. Pollifax. "Where are Hanan and Qasim?"

"They left at once by camel to assure Hanan's grandfather they are well and

that we reached you in time. The child Hanan—''

"Not such a child," said Farrell dryly.

"—seems most fond of you, Mrs. Pollifax." He smiled ironically. "She pointed
out very firmly that neither you nor Mr.
Farrell were in any condition to walk
twelve kilometers to the plane, and that
she and Joseph will return with a truck
and many mattresses to take you back to
her grandfather's camp."

"Oh yes," Mrs. Pollifax said firmly, "I
would insist on that."

"Oh?" responded the inspector, with a
lift of an eyebrow. "Not back with us to
Amman?"

Farrell said grimly, "Duchess, we have
a plane to catch!"

"But Farrell," she said earnestly, "we
can't leave without paying our respects to
the sheikh—or seeing Hanan and Joseph
again. I insist!" Ignoring Farrell's frown,
she said to the inspector, "Take Farrell
back with you, he's the more badly hurt;
my arm is much better, and I'll be quite
safe, staying here and waiting for them."

"Not on your life, Duchess," Farrell told
her indignantly. "If you stay, I stay."

"Well, then," she told the inspector, "we will *both* of us retrieve our guide, Joseph—his car should have a battery by now—and thank the sheikh for his hospitality. While we wait, we can watch the sun rise and we can rest."

"I could order an army helicopter for you," Jafer said.

"Please no," she told him firmly, and tried standing; she was only a little dizzy.

"But you both need medical attention," he protested.

She smiled. "You are very kind, but personally, I cannot leave the desert without seeing Joseph and Hanan."

He shrugged. "As you wish, we've much to do as it is." With a glance at the helicopter, he rose. "They're bringing Taimour out now. *Afwan,*" and with a glance at the sky, "Nearing time for the Azan."

"The what?"

"Call to prayer," he said, and strode away.

Watching them carry Taimour to the helicopter, heavily wrapped in blankets, Mrs. Pollifax sighed. "I feel I *cannot* be sorry I hit Mr. Taimour so hard, not after what he's done to you—and I do prefer being alive, which I doubt I would be now, because who knows if Inspector Jafer would have arrived in time?"

"You didn't *kill* him, Duchess," pointed out Farrell gently, "and the inspector said he's going to survive. Consider *my* gratitude instead, Duchess, although I'm wondering how many days it will be until I can lie on my back."

She said with authority, "For several days you will have to lie on your stomach, but after a little while you'll be able to lie flat on your back on a fur rug or a mat of sheep's wool."

He looked at her in surprise. "Duchess—you, too?"

She nodded. "Hong Kong."

"Well I'm damn sorry I got you into this," he said flatly, "but I hope you realize that without you I would now be the late John Sebastian Farrell, and your encounter with Mr. Nayef has not been unproductive either. It's getting monotonous, Duchess, you saved my life in Albania—"

"Yes, but you saved Cyrus's and my life in Zambia."

"True, but in Sicily—"

The roar of the helicopter's engine blighted any further exchange. "I think we should get out of the way," shouted Mrs. Pollifax, and helped him to his feet.

They stood and watched the inspector and two of his men push the helicopter free of the great arched roof of the castle. Once outside the pilot leaned from the window, shouted something, gave a thumbs-up signal, and the blades began to turn. Faster and faster they gyrated, slowly lifting the helicopter from the ground; after which it gained speed, swerved to the east, and flew out of sight behind the castle, the noise of it slowly receding.

From somewhere Inspector Jafer produced two plastic cups of water, and Mrs. Pollifax and Farrell sat and gratefully sipped from them as they watched the horizon turn gray and then silver. When the inspector's plane arrived they had this to watch too: it circled the castle, then began a landing on the flat stony desert floor, pulled up to try again, and at last ground to a bumpy halt on land. A tightly roped and handcuffed Mr. Nayef, otherwise known as Suhair Slaman, was led out of the castle under guard and escorted down the hill to the plane in the company of more men than Mrs. Pollifax had realized were present.

The inspector stopped to speak to them. "You will see me again in Amman," he said, and with a faint smile, "It has been a pleasure meeting two such—such *professional* people, should I say? We are in your debt. You will be all right?"

"I just want to sleep," confided Mrs. Pollifax, "until Hanan comes."

"Then I wish you a good sleep," he said gravely, and began his walk to the plane below.

20

Mrs. Pollifax sat with her back to the wall of the castle's great banquet hall and watched the sun approach the horizon, preceded by a glorious burst of gold and crimson, and then, abruptly, the sun emerged, a huge globe of orange, and for just a moment the flint stones in the desert glittered silver. Overhead she could hear the rustling of bats, newly returned from their night out and no doubt annoyed by these two intruders. She had spread out her blanket for Farrell and he lay across it on his stomach, but she knew he couldn't sleep. She was sorry she'd not more forcibly insisted that he leave with the inspector on the plane; he had been anointed with a variety of oils—very biblical, he'd added—but she knew he must still be in pain. He would need more than Joseph's taxi to return him to Amman.

She sighed, closed her eyes, and for a few minutes slept, but uneasily, with strange shapes and the face of Taimour haunting her. She opened her eyes and looked at her watch. "Farrell, they should be coming for us soon."

"Yes. Help me up," he said. "Standing's better."

"What did they give you, anything more than ointments?"

"Oh yes—two shots," he said. "Tetanus and something for the pain." He shivered.

"Try not to think back," she counseled. "Try, do try."

He nodded. "I'm trying."

As they limped wearily out of the shadowed castle into the heat and sun, they could see around them for miles. The Wadi Ghaduf followed its serpentine route north, and then, turning to the south, they could see in the distance three tall columns of rock, like cones, interrupting a desert utterly empty except for small islands of grass. The air was so clear that in the west Mrs. Pollifax could even make out a dark smudge of tiny shapes that could be the sheikh's camp, reduced by Hanan's fifteen kilometers to black dots on a tawny landscape. There was a faint warm breeze, but otherwise nothing stirred.

"A lonely place," murmured Farrell.

"But a pleasing loneliness," said Mrs. Pollifax.

"Thanks, but I prefer cities, smog, and people. How's your arm?"

"Not bad. How's your back?"

He gave her a humorous glance. "Not bad."

"You tell lies well," she said.

"So do you, Duchess."

They were silent, looking out on the great stillness, the emptiness that to Mrs. Pollifax was not quite emptiness but something timeless and so full of space that it rested her eyes, her heart, and possibly, she thought, her soul. It would be this that she would remember, she knew; not Mr. Nayef or Taimour or the violence, but this space and silence and the hospitality of the Bedouin—*and Hanan,* she added with a smile.

Beside her she heard Farrell sigh. He

said, "We've gone through hell with your Mr. Nayef and my Iraqi friend, and that's behind us now, but unfortunately with the dawn comes reality, and for myself, damn it, I've still failed. No Ibrahim."

"Which reminds me of something I've not mentioned," she said, "it's been such a busy night. It's not *quite* a failure, dear Farrell."

"What is it you've not mentioned?" he said crossly. "And *don't* try to console me."

Mrs. Pollifax smiled. "I wouldn't offer consolation for the world, Farrell, but I *think* you'll find Ibrahim back at the camp."

"I'll *what*?" He turned and stared at her.

"I said that I think you'll find Ibrahim, after all—at the tent of Hanan's grandfather."

He looked worried. "Are you all right, Duchess? You've gone through a hell of a night, is this something you dreamed while you were asleep?"

"While I slept I had nightmares, not dreams," she said tartly. "I repeat: I *think* you will find Ibrahim back at the sheikh's camp."

"My God, Duchess," he said, "how can you say that, how can you know?"

"We both knew," she said, remembering. "He sat down across the campfire from me in the tent and he stared at me, frowning and puzzled, and I looked at him, and then—quite suddenly, we both knew."

"Knew what?"

"That he was the man who rushed past me at Karak castle, and I was the woman who was standing by the wall."

"Did *I* see this man?" he demanded.

She shook her head. "You'd gone out to look at the stars."

"But you couldn't even describe him to the police!" he said accusingly.

"I couldn't, no," she admitted, "but how could I have described to them what was only an impression? And yet—in some strange way—would *subliminally* be the word?—I was more conscious of what I saw than I realized. . . . I *knew.*"

"But at the sheikh's tent, of all places?"

She said calmly, "I believe he must be one of the men they spoke of finding in the desert a month ago, nearly dead from thirst."

"But why—?"

"Are you forgetting how close we are to the Saudi border?" she reminded him. "We didn't know that until tonight—or was it yesterday. You said yourself a century ago, back in the hotel on our first night here, that Ibrahim might have to come this way, skirting the Iraq-Saudi border."

Farrell looked stunned. "My God, Duchess, if you're right—" His voice was shaken. "I shall pray all the way back to the camp."

"I think you can begin your prayers now," she said, pointing. "There's a cloud of dust off to the west, and it's moving in our direction, it must surely be Awad's truck coming for us."

But it was another forty minutes before the truck could be seen in detail, and another ten minutes before it came to a stop below the rise on which the castle stood.

"I hope it doesn't bounce too much," Farrell said nervously.

"Hanan promised mattresses, remember?"

What Mrs. Pollifax had not considered was Joseph's youth and pride. As he rushed up the hill to them she feared for a moment that he was going to throw himself at her feet with apologies; they were on his tour, he said, his responsibility, his friends, and that such harm had come to them devastated him, he would return their money to them, he would—but Hanan spoke chidingly to him, reminding him they were hurt, and when he was silenced Mrs. Pollifax said, with a smile, "Don't you dare spoil such a welcome rescue!"

Joseph then turned to Farrell and spoke eagerly of the care with which he would be returned to his grandfather's camp and, taking him by the arm, helped him down to the truck. "As if," said Farrell dryly, "I'm one hundred years old."

Every pillow from the sheikh's tent appeared to have been stuffed into the open rear of the truck, as well as five mattresses. Farrell was placed among them, with Hanan to keep them secure during the drive. Mrs. Pollifax, her arm still wrapped in Taimour's striped silk, was given the front seat next to Joseph. In this manner they began their return to the camp, which they had left—to Mrs. Pollifax's surprise—only twelve hours ago.

21

Once again they sat around the fire in the sheikh's tent, although Farrell had seated himself awkwardly on the low table that held coffee urns and the radio. His back had been examined by a little man named Bushaq—Hanan confiding to Mrs. Pollifax that he had all the gifts of a *taheeb,* or doctor—and then Mrs. Pollifax's arm had been unwrapped by Bushaq, who amused her because she had not seen a Bedouin wearing spectacles before, and she found this oddly endearing. Pressing and probing he had announced—Hanan had to translate, for he did not speak English—that no bullet had remained in her arm, but she had lost both flesh and blood, after which he had fashioned a sling for her and ordered rich broth for her to drink.

It was the ubiquitous coffee that was being served now in small cups. A sandstorm had sprung up since their arrival and with it a strong wind that beat against the sides of the *bait sha'ar* and played with the flames in the fire pit.

"We must talk now," Farrell said to Joseph's grandfather. He had said this upon their arrival, but Sheikh Jidoor had paid no attention. Now he bowed his head and waited.

Farrell glanced at Mrs. Pollifax and said, "You begin, Duchess, you're the one who was so *sure.*"

"But delicately," she reminded him, and to Sheikh Jidoor she said very casually, "Sir, you spoke of finding a small party of men in the desert some time ago. In great trouble, and one of them dead."

The sheikh looked at her without expression. *"Na'am."*

"We would like to ask you, Mr. Farrell and I, if one of them might be named Ibrahim?"

He conferred briefly with the man beside him. "No," he said.

She heard Farrell swear softly under his breath.

"Then may I ask what their first names are?" she persisted.

His voice was curt. "Mustafa and Dalshad."

She did not comment on this. She said, "I think one of the men came into the tent last night, when the boy was playing the *rababa,* for his cheekbones were white, as if the skin had been peeled away by the sun."

The sheikh's eyes narrowed, but he said nothing.

"May we see that man?" she asked.

The sheikh only smiled politely, as if he'd not heard her.

Stubbornly Mrs. Pollifax continued. "Did one of them by any chance make a trip to Karak castle with a young boy on a donkey, camping there overnight?"

From his corner in the shadows she heard Joseph catch his breath.

Farrell stared at her in surprise, and with a cryptic smile she said, "I've had time to think. To put two and two together, my friend."

The sheikh said, in a harsh voice, "You

came here with Youseff, Hanan, and Awad Ibn Jazi to visit a fort. Why do you suddenly interest yourself in these men, you wish them harm?"

"In our search for a man named Ibrahim," she told him, "it is *we* who have come to harm." She pointed to her arm. "We had given up our search when we came here. Joseph knows of this."

The sheikh's head turned toward the shadows, and Joseph nodded. "They speak truth. There was no reason to tell of it here, and I promised them my silence."

Farrell spoke now. "I would ask two questions, sir. Did these men from the desert hear of a Farrell being dragged away from the camp in the night?"

"No," said Sheikh Jidoor. "They are in a tent removed from the others, for quiet and for healing."

"Then I would next ask, sir, if you could speak to the men Mustafa and Dalshad, and ask them if the name of Farrell is known to them."

The sheikh bowed courteously. "I could do that, yes." He spoke to the man beside him, who rose and went out.

Mrs. Pollifax and Farrell exchanged

glances. In a low voice she said, "He's protecting them, isn't he?"

Farrell nodded. "He certainly doesn't want us to know about them, whoever they are."

"Do you think I've violated some tribal law, asking about his guests? If I have," she said anxiously, "then—"

"Wait," said Farrell sharply, and pointed.

The man with the scarred white cheekbones was being ushered inside. When his gaze met Mrs. Pollifax's he came to an abrupt stop and suddenly smiled. *"You,"* he said.

She smiled back at him warmly. "Yes."

His glance moved quickly to Farrell, and then as quickly returned to his host. *"As salam alaikum!"* he murmured.

Sheikh Jidoor had risen, and he bowed slightly. *"Alaikum as salam!"*

Speaking in excellent English his guest said, "And you are well?"

"I am well, praise be to God," replied the sheikh.

"On you be peace."

"And may *you* be well," returned the sheikh.

Mrs. Pollifax could almost taste Farrell's impatience; he looked exasperated.

"What God willeth," said the man, with a shrug.

The sheikh smiled. "God keep you," and then, "You must have coffee. Please sit."

The sheikh seated himself, but the man remained standing, his gaze widening to include Farrell. "You are the man Farrell?" he asked.

Farrell nodded. "Yes, and you—am I meeting Ibrahim at last?"

"It is a name familiar to me," he said cautiously.

"Then we have each come a long way to meet," Farrell told him politely, "and I hope you are Ibrahim, who brings me something of value from a mutual friend."

The man's eyes remained fixed on Farrell's face doubtfully and Mrs. Pollifax sighed. Feeling that each of them needed prodding, she intervened, saying bluntly, "You didn't kill the Iraqi, you know; your blood was on his dagger but there was no blood on him—except, of course, on the back of his head where he hit the wall. The police must know that by now. And we are very sorry to hear that one of the men with you died in the desert."

He looked amused at this outburst, and his face softened. To Farrell he said, "It is hard to trust—and you have no mustache. I have seen pictures, you understand? But yes, I am Ibrahim."

Hallelujah, murmured Mrs. Pollifax.

"So that's it," Farrell said, and reaching into an inner pocket of his jacket, he brought out a snapshot, a picture of himself. "Damn risky to have brought this," he added. Painfully he removed himself from the table and carried it to Ibrahim. "I've a mustache in this one. Does this help?"

Ibrahim glanced at the photo and smiled. "Very much. The two of you, yes, but it *was* risky."

The sheikh, who had been following this, frowned and said, "You are not Mustafa, then, but Ibrahim?"

With a wry smile, Ibrahim said, "Forgive me, but to be honest I am neither." Returning the photo he said, "You have both, the two of you . . . but come to the tent the sheikh has so kindly allowed us."

Mrs. Pollifax followed him and Farrell

outside and discovered the wind no longer scattering pebbles and debris through the camp; the sandstorm had subsided, and in the east a patch of blue sky had appeared. As they walked toward the outer fringe of the camp, to the secluded tent at the far end, Ibrahim said gravely, "You understand there were many losses on our journey across the desert. We had nothing—*nothing*—neither camels nor food nor baggage when we were found."

Farrell said impatiently, "Yes, but you do have the manuscript with you, and safe."

Ibrahim hesitated, then stopped and turned to face him. "I'm sorry. *Very* sorry, Mr. Farrell."

"You can't mean—what do you *mean*?" demanded Farrell. "It's here, isn't it, you have it with you, you kept it safe, you brought it out?"

Very gently Ibrahim said, "Near the end, Mr. Farrell, we were barely alive, and the nights were long and cold. We had no fuel except shreds of our clothing and dried camel dung and three or four matches. We desperately needed kindling. To keep alive—and we were very weak—we needed fire."

"Oh *no,*" gasped Farrell.

"Yes." Ibrahim nodded. "The pages of the manuscript started *good* fires for us."

Farrell groaned.

Ibrahim added, "But the loss is not unrepairable."

"What do you mean, 'not unrepairable'? How can you say that?" said Farrell bitterly, and Mrs. Pollifax knew that he was thinking of the long way he had come for this, and of the welts on his back, but she wished he might curb his anger.

Ibrahim only said gravely, "Come," and he pulled up the flap of the tent and held it for them both to enter.

It was dark inside, except for a small lantern beside a couch built of many carpets on which a man lay sleeping. The light illuminated only half of his face: a wiry black beard, the jut of a nose, a head of black hair threaded with gray.

Ibrahim said, "Now you see why the Iraqi *mukhabarat* have absolutely had to find us. To kill."

"My God," breathed Farrell, staring. "Dib Assen—and *alive*?"

The man on the couch stirred, opened his eyes, and regarded them with surprise. Puzzled, he said, "Who—" and he whispered, "It can't be," and then with a roar of delight, *"Farrell!"*

Mrs. Pollifax touched Ibrahim's arm. "Come," she said softly, drawing him out of the tent into the sun. "I think for a few minutes we don't belong there, and tell me, Ibrahim, *tell me! Like Lazarus he's risen from the dead, but please, can you explain how? You must* know that his death has been announced in newspapers all over Europe and America!"

The sun was harsh after the darkness of the tent, and Ibrahim's voice was equally as harsh. "Explain?" he said. "Think back? So many miles ago?" He shook his head. "So *many* miles ago! But a Lazarus should be explained, yes."

He stared silently into the desert as if willing himself to remember. "They were so complacent," he began. "How could he hide or escape in a country with so many informers? And he so well known? They had arrested him before, and Assen *never* hid.

"But still there are a few," he said

softly. "Brave, brave people. One of them worked at—he had known Assen once—but I say no more."

He did not speak easily; there was a weariness in him that she hoped she would never know, and she waited patiently.

When he spoke again he said, "They had such confidence—such conceit! They announced they had arrested him even before they set out to arrest him, and why not? Where could he go? But he had been warned—barely. Minutes before they reached his house he left. Three of us. To escape. You can imagine the fury? and their embarrassment? the blow to their conceit?

"To cover their failure—their bungling—it was cunning of them—they announced his death. But of course," he added simply, "they knew he would be dead soon enough."

"Except he survived."

"Yes."

They were silent, and then Ibrahim said, "He was very near to death when we were found, and he is not strong even yet—or safe."

"Is he well enough to leave?"

Ibrahim gestured helplessly. "To go where? The *mukhabarat* have long arms. To Amman? There are many defectors from Iraq in Jordan—thousands, fine people—but can any of them, can *anyone,* protect him from secret police across the border?"

"His book," said Mrs. Pollifax, frowning, "did it really hold secret information they'd not want known?"

He nodded. "Oh yes. I've not had the honor of reading it—it had been hidden away, and in the desert who can read?—but he has told me—as we walked in the desert—how he plotted his story in villages—locations—*real* places where he'd learned there are secret factories hidden from the United Nations inspectors, and in his book he named what was being manufactured, using code. Botulinum toxin near one village, and in another the toxin ricin . . . They kill horribly. Now the book is gone, he carries it in his mind, and he has to be hunted down and destroyed."

"He mustn't be," she said passionately, "he must come to the United States, except—" She stopped, suddenly perplexed. "Except how to get him out without *help*? Even to Amman without risk, without his being seen and known or caught. He doesn't have a passport, does he?"

Ibrahim looked at her pityingly. "From Iraq? No passports."

She shook her head. "What we need, then," she said sadly, "is an angel of deliverance."

"A *what*?"

"Angels," she said, "are very big now in the United States; they write books about them. It's said they bring miracles, such as how to smuggle a wanted man out of a strange country. Without passport or visa."

"There are no miracles," he said flatly.

"Dib Assen being still alive is a miracle," she said defiantly. "And *you're* alive."

"Yes, but—" He suddenly stiffened, and she saw his face contort with dread. "*Bismallah*—oh *Bismallah,* look—I must not be *seen!*"

"What is it?" she cried, but he had rushed around the corner of the tent to hide himself. Turning to look in the opposite direction she saw what looked like a Land Rover, very dusty and with huge tires, making its way into the camp. It came to a stop at the sheikh's tent. To see such a modern vehicle was a sudden shock to the eye, the reminder of a very different world beyond the desert of shabby pickup trucks and camels. She turned to Ibrahim, who knelt on the ground out of sight. "What is it? *Who* is it?" she asked.

"Desert Patrol. Two men, you see them? Police!"

Oh God, thought Mrs. Pollifax. She watched the two men climb out of the car, and there was no doubt that one of them was a member of the desert police because he wore the trim brown uniform with brown belts crossing his chest and a red arm sash circling his shoulder. His red-checked *kaffiyeh* was bound with a dark *aigal,* on which was pinned a silver badge. The man with him was in civilian clothes, young and dusty, but looking very official.

Both disappeared into the sheikh's tent.

Mrs. Pollifax waited, but for what she didn't know: a polite request to search the tents, perhaps, or news of a dangerous man in hiding nearby? Her arm was throbbing, she'd had no sleep, and her head had begun to ache. *I ought to warn Farrell,* she thought, but she felt paralyzed and very, very tired.

Over her shoulder she told Ibrahim, "They've gone into the tent of Sheikh Jidoor."

"Yes," he said in a strangled voice.

A flap in the sheikh's tent opened and she braced herself, but it was only young Joseph who emerged. Seeing her he waved and ran toward her, looking excited. "Mrs. Pollifax," he shouted, "the Desert Patrol has brought in a man lost in the desert last night! He is American and he is asking for you!"

This was bewildering. "Asking for *me*? An *American* asking for me?"

"Yes," cried Joseph. "Corporal Saidi found him last night near the Saudi border, very lost. His name is Rollin or Rallin or Rawling, and he says a Mr. Carstairs sent him."

Carstairs . . . ! Her knees felt suddenly weak. Battered and bruised, she experienced the strangest longing to burst into tears but instead she laughed. It was a shaky laugh, but it was a laugh. "Ibrahim," she said, "you can stop hiding now, I think our angel of deliverance has just arrived . . . our miracle."

Which, if Carstairs could have heard this, would have provoked an explosion of incredulous and pithy comments.

Epilogue

Mrs. Pollifax had been at home for four days before news reached her of arrangements made in Amman after she and Farrell left. Cyrus had already returned from the Cape when she arrived, and she was greeted at the door with a horrified, "Good God, Emily, a broken arm?"

"No, no," she told him reassuringly, "it's only a small bullet wound. A Bedouin named Bushaq treated it, and a handsome young policeman disinfected it."

He eyed her suspiciously. "Emily, a bullet implies a gun, and on the phone you said—"

"There were complications," she admitted, and after a brief summation of her week in Jordan and an inquiry about his bird-watching expedition, she went to bed and slept for ten hours. This was dull but welcome, since she'd not slept on the plane or the night before, but once she awoke she began to want very much to hear news of what was happening to Assen and Ibrahim. Rawlings had promised her news. . . . *A very nice young man, Rawlings,* she thought, and almost abject in his gratitude to her for what he had experienced in the desert. "It was an *adventure,*" he told her. "Absolutely thrilling. There was a moon, you know—I had no idea what I'd been missing!"

She had refrained from mentioning what could have happened to him if his car had broken down in a less-patrolled area of the desert. Presumably he would learn this in time, since he gave every evidence of wanting to explore the desert further. She had given him Awad Ibn Jazi's name, emphasizing how interesting Rawlings would find him, and she hoped he would have the sense to contact him.

It was Tuesday when she had returned from Jordan; it was Saturday when Bishop called from New York to say that if she and Cyrus were at home that afternoon, he would like to drive to Connecticut and see them. He had a small package for her, he added, that was too important to mail.

"I hope not an Urn Tomb," was Cyrus's cryptic response.

Bishop arrived promptly at two o'clock, attaché case in hand and looking as boyish as usual, his sandy hair concealed under a jaunty plaid cap, which he removed with a flourish. Bishop liked kitchens, explaining that he rarely saw any, and so they established themselves at the kitchen table with blueberry muffins and a carafe of coffee. It was apparent to Mrs. Pollifax that pleasantries had to be exchanged first, and she wondered if this was Bishop's way of commiserating with Cyrus at his missing his wife's fun and games in Jordan. This amused her enough to curb her impatience.

Bishop said, "I liked that girl Kadi Hopkirk; I hear you took her bird-watching."

Cyrus nodded. "A damn good sport, but raised in too hot a climate. Shivers a lot. Always cold. Not sure I converted her to bird-watching," he said doubtfully. "Too much fresh air, perhaps."

"You certainly look healthy," Bishop told him. "It obviously agreed with *you*."

"Of course I look healthy," growled Cyrus, "I didn't go flying off to the Middle East to cope with a bunch of felons and get shot in the arm. Very devious woman, my wife," he told Bishop. "Phoned to tell me she was going off with Farrell for a week, to bring back some documents or some such from Jordan. Courier work, I thought. Comes home exhausted and with her arm in a sling."

"Devious indeed," said Bishop with a grin.

Mrs. Pollifax could be patient no longer. "Bishop, what's been happening?" she asked. "Have you heard yet, are they all right?"

Bishop nodded. "I bear good news, yes. You'll be glad to hear that with a great deal of cooperation in Amman, we brought Assen and Ibrahim to the United States yesterday. His information's being turned over to the UN—as well as shared with Jordan," he added, "and damn important it is. He's now in a safe house."

"I'm certainly relieved to hear that," she told him.

"Real sacrifice, that manuscript," put in Cyrus. "I've read both *Plague of Demons* and *Instruments of Torture* . . . valuable books. Can he reconstruct from memory this book that's been destroyed?"

"I doubt he'll want to now," said Bishop. "Now that he's free to say and write what he wants, and he no longer has to hide truths behind metaphors and anagrams and veiled hints and references."

"But you're sure he's safe?" asked Mrs. Pollifax.

Bishop grinned. "He's so safe that neither Carstairs nor I know where he is. Only Antun Mahmoud knows—and the FBI, who have given him a new identity."

"Not even Farrell?"

"Not even Farrell."

"And Ibrahim?"

"Ibrahim continued on to Mexico to join Farrell; it seems that he's an expert on Islamic art, so they have rather a lot in common. Dib Assen hopes to move there, too, once the FBI allows it. In the meantime he has a visa for six months and is eligible for political refugee status if he prefers to stay, but in any case he is being very well guarded for the moment. As to Farrell," he added gravely, "we are reimbursing him for all of his expenses; he went as Assen's friend but brought back to us more than we dreamed possible." He winced. "But I'm overlooking what brings me here, specifically this package that arrived through official channels, by courier and sans customs, with the request that it be promptly delivered to you."

Puzzled, Mrs. Pollifax said, "What can that be?"

"It's from the palace in Amman. No message. Simply that it comes from the palace." Opening his attaché case he presented her with a long and slender package wrapped in brown paper. After fumbling with the strings she found a tissue-wrapped box and, opening it, said, "But how kind!" and then, "Oh dear!"

It was a dagger, its scabbard turquoise studded, very old and very beautiful, its handle circled with gems and insets of gold. Reluctantly she drew the dagger from its sheath.

Cyrus said, "Oh-oh!"

Bishop whistled through his teeth and said, "Gorgeous. A real museum piece!" and then, after a glance at her face,

"What's up? You don't look terribly happy to see it."

She said weakly, "A dagger like this came very near to slitting my throat last Saturday just seven days ago at the Qasr at Tūba. Less ornate, of course, but just as sharp." She shivered. "Mr. Nayef—sorry, Mr. Slaman—was a *very* determined man."

"Ouch," said Bishop. "But this dagger must be hundreds of years old—a real antique—and it's *royal.* You can't ignore it, and it simply wouldn't do to slice tomatoes with it."

"This does make it all a bit tricky," Cyrus said thoughtfully. "I think an attitude is needed, m'dear. After all, from the palace—"

"And so beautiful," said Bishop. "How about displaying it to remind you of the dagger that nearly did but didn't?"

She gave him a reproachful glance, and then, running her fingers over the exquisite carvings on the scabbard, she admitted that it was indeed beautiful. "I'm sure that it's Bedouin," she said, and with a smile, "A pity I can't share it with Hanan. *Wellahi hadha, beduwi*—a real *bedu*!"

"You've already sent her a complete set of Nancy Drew mysteries," pointed out Cyrus.

"*I've* thought of an attitude," said Bishop suddenly, with his usual flippancy. "Hang it on a wall as a reminder to beware of the person seated beside you on your next plane trip."

"No need," Cyrus said firmly. "Next time, damn it—and I want her promise on this—it'll be *me* sitting next to her."

ABOUT THE AUTHOR

DOROTHY GILMAN is the author of twelve earlier Mrs. Pollifax novels, including *The Unexpected Mrs. Pollifax* (the series debut), *The Amazing Mrs. Pollifax, Mrs. Pollifax Pursued,* and *Mrs. Pollifax and the Lion Killer.* She lives in Westport, Connecticut, and Albuquerque, New Mexico.